I0760925

The Body in the Road

To my sister

A Craven Falls Mystery

Book 3

The Body in the Road

Donna M. Zadunajsky

The Body in the Road

www.donnazadunajsky.com

ISBN: Hardcover: 978-1-938037-81-8
ISBN: eBook: 978-1-938037-89-4
ISBN: Paperback: 979-8-732258-08-0

Printed in the United States of America.

Chapter 1

Sara Nelson's knuckles turned a shade of white as she gripped the hard, black steering wheel wrapped tightly under her fingers. The wipers whipped back and forth as the rain, or should she say *buckets of water*, because if it was just raindrops coming down from the sky, then she could see the road. But that was the problem. She couldn't see the road in front of her. She couldn't see any farther than the emblem that sat mounted on the hood of her car.

The same emblem that was swallowed by the darkness as she drove *her* apple-red 1958 Cadillac Eldorado down the murky, wooded road, heading to where—she wasn't sure. Technically, it was *her* car—now. Her grandmother had left it to Sara in her will. She just wasn't dead yet, but what did it matter? It would eventually be hers.

The rain froze in midair, like hitting pause on the TV, stopping long enough for Sara to see a sign come into view that read: WELCOME TO CRAVEN FALLS.

She had never heard of this town, Craven Falls, and she had lived in Ohio her entire life. Well, seventeen years, because that's how old she was. She hadn't even completed high school yet; no thanks to that asshole ex-boyfriend, Brad, who didn't even know they broke up as of today. Nope, she had just packed her things and taken off in the middle of the night in her grandmother's car.

She left no note.

She told no one.

She got in the car and drove out of the driveway, heading south, as far away from Brad as she could get. She knew that if she didn't leave, she would be next. He would find her, and he would kill her.

The rain intensified once more, heavier than it had been before. She prayed there was a motel nearby where she could stop for the night, but she saw nothing—no houses or stores. She was in the middle of freaking nowhere, facing what felt like a typhoon approaching her.

The wind was pushing and shoving her car, like a bully did to a harmless kid half their size. Well, that's how it felt from inside the vehicle, anyway. She was just thankful she didn't get motion sickness, the way the car seemed to sway each time a gust of wind slammed against its frame.

She loosened her grip on the steering wheel, wiggling her now swollen fingers so blood could flow back into them, making them thin again. She rolled her shoulders back to relieve the tension balling up between each vertebrae. The muscles in her neck were tight, and she felt a headache surfacing as it inched its way up the back of her skull. The roots of her hair tingled. She lifted one hand from the steering wheel and rubbed the back right side of her head near the edge of the skull. The pain subsided.

Her mind bounced from one thing to another, though she was sure it was because of the stress and anxiety she was under. At that moment, she wondered what would happen if she ran out of gas on this dark, isolated, wooded road. She took her eyes off the road and looked down at the gas gauge to see how much gas she had left. She still had half a tank.

"Thank God," she whispered.

Her eyes shifted from the dashboard to the road and then

back down at the dashboard, almost missing an object in the road. She took her foot off the gas pedal to slow the car down, though she wasn't going fast to begin with. She pressed her foot on the brake, released it, and pressed down again. She didn't want the car to spin out of control when the roads were wet, as her grandmother had advised her when she started driving last year.

She wasn't sure what she was seeing. Was the rain causing her to see things that weren't really there? It was dark outside, which didn't help at all. Or, as her mind considered every possible scenario, it was because she was utterly exhausted from the fear of Brad finding her.

Coming after her.

She knew that if he found her, she would never see her family again. He would make sure of that. She shook the thoughts away. Now wasn't the time to be thinking of what he would do to her if he found her, because she would not let him find her.

She slowed the car to a crawl and leaned over the steering wheel for a better view through the windshield. The rain blurred her vision, making it difficult to see, and the road seemed to grow darker the further she drove into the woods. It was also possible that her mind was playing tricks on her; she was sure of this since she saw nothing.

She pressed on the gas just as the mist rose from the asphalt and drifted away. Was it an animal? Maybe a deer? Yes, someone had hit a deer and left it lying in the road instead of moving it to the side, away from oncoming traffic. Not that there was a lot of traffic on this road; actually, there was none. No one was stupid enough to be out driving in this weather, except for her.

She was certain she saw something up ahead. She leaned in closer, the hard steering wheel pressing into her ribs. Yet, she still couldn't tell what exactly it was. The harder the rain fell, the more steam rose from the blacktop.

Sara approached what looked like an animal, navigating her car away from the object and off the side of the road. She stopped and put the car in park, turning on her hazards so the other drivers could see her vehicle. She looked out the driver's side window but couldn't see anything. She wiped away the moisture covering the glass caused by her heavy breathing.

On the ground lay not an animal, but a body.

Chapter 2

"A body," she gasped.

Yes, her mind confirmed a body, as if she were doubting herself.

"What would a body be doing out here on a night like tonight?" she whispered. But then again, why did it matter what night it was?

Sara squinted. She couldn't tell if the person was a man or a woman. For a moment, she thought it could be a child, or maybe even a teenager. Her eyes moved down the body. The body was sprawled out, one leg bent at an angle. She didn't have to be a doctor to know that the leg was broken, snapped in half like a twig, and the other leg bent toward the person's chest. Oddly, this made her think about the way she slept, with one leg bent toward her chest and the other straight out behind her. Half on her side, half on her belly. Why would she even think about something like that? Someone was lying on the road.

In the pouring rain.

Possibly dead.

In the middle of freaking nowhere.

And she was thinking about how she slept with one leg bent? What was wrong with her? Was she finally losing it? Showing no remorse for the living or the dead? Had Brad finally turned her into him? Some evil person? Someone who didn't give a shit anymore.

"No, of course not," she retorted, feeling mortified for even thinking such a thing. She was nothing like him. She never would be. It was just the way the body was lying on the road that reminded her of how she slept. Stupid, yes! But that was how she sometimes thought.

She jiggled the thoughts from her head and stared back out the window. She had to re-wipe the window clean, as her breath had fogged up the glass again. She saw one arm laid above the person's head and the other by their face.

The face was difficult to recognize from her position in the car, about ten or possibly twenty feet away, and the ongoing rain didn't help either. If she could see the face clearly, then she would discern whether it was female or male, young or old.

She wanted to get out and help the person, but she knew by looking at them that they weren't breathing, weren't alive. But she wasn't certain. How could she help them if they were already dead? She could call for help. Yes, that's exactly what she should do or should have done already, but she hadn't because she was too busy wondering what gender the person was.

She could call in the body and leave. She would find a place to stay for the night and hit the road before dawn. She wasn't sure why her mind had already decided that she would leave the scene after notifying the police about the body in the road.

Why would she leave?

Why should she stay? Her mind disputed.

Why the hell was she arguing with herself?

She felt stupid and annoyed with herself for acting like an inconsiderate, spoiled brat. She would wait here until the police arrived. It was the right thing to do. Besides, she had nowhere to be, except maybe in a warm bed, because she was dog-tired. Perhaps that's why she was having these thoughts? Her brain was clogged, and she couldn't think straight. But still, it plagued her that she would leave this poor person lying here in the rain, instead of staying and waiting for someone to arrive and take the body to the morgue or even the hospital.

The person was probably dead, but she didn't want to leave the body here for the animals to come and... she couldn't even finish the thought. Why would she think about what the animals would do to the body? Yes, she was in the woods, and animals of all kinds lived there. But that didn't mean that they, the animals, would come out in the pouring rain and devour this poor, lifeless person.

Again, she was disgusted by her thoughts. This wasn't like her. Her mind had never considered things like this. Though she had never been in a situation like this before, and thank God for that. How often does a person encounter a dead body? And one lying in the road where no houses or commercial buildings are around for miles?

Did this make her a bad person for thinking all these things? She used to be a good person. No! She was still a good person. She just had issues that she was battling at this moment.

Sara reached for her cell phone, which she had placed inside the glove box, and turned it on. She had powered the phone down so she wouldn't hear Brad trying to call her and because he would track her once he discovered she had left.

The white apple appeared on the screen as it came to life. She used her thumbprint to unlock the screen. The second the home screen appeared, she saw that she had twenty missed calls and nineteen voicemails. She didn't have to be a mind reader to know that they were probably all from Brad. How had he known that she had left so fast? Had he followed her home? How? She made sure that he wasn't watching her. But this was what Brad did. He'd call her to confirm she was home and not out with anyone else. Or out driving in a thunderstorm in the middle of God knows where, like she was doing this very minute.

She knew that if she didn't answer his calls, he would drive over to her house, if he wasn't there already, sitting outside, watching. Sara was glad that he wouldn't notice the Eldorado missing because they always kept it inside the garage, unless he looked inside. *Would he do that?* Yes, she knew he would.

She opened the phone icon and dialed 9-1-1, but the call didn't go through. She glanced at the top right corner of the screen and noticed she had no service. No bars meant she couldn't make calls.

She couldn't call for help.

She was in a dead zone.

"Great!" she fumed. "Now what?"

If she couldn't call for help, then she was this person's only hope. Sara powered down the phone and placed it back inside the glove compartment. She knew that Brad could track her if he wanted to. But then again, all she had to do was turn off *Find My Phone,* and he wouldn't be able to find her, right? She didn't know, but she hoped it was that simple. *She would do it later,* she thought. *Right now, she had other things to deal with.*

She turned and looked back out the window. The body remained in the same position it had occupied for the past two minutes. *Of course, it was*. Did she think that the person would get up and walk away? That they were playing a practical joke on anyone who drove by? She wanted to laugh out loud but didn't find it particularly amusing. This was no joke or game. The person was dead, and she was sitting here doing nothing. Well, she tried to call for help, but that didn't happen because there was no cell service.

She needed to consider her options. Should she drive away like the person who had hit the body lying in the road had? Though she didn't know for sure if a car had hit the body, did she? Maybe they were running and fell right there in the middle of the road.

Sara laughed. The sound bounced all around her in the empty car. Not that she found it amusing. It wasn't funny. She was imagining the person running and falling right there as if it were a soft mattress to fall on. And then didn't get back up. Just laid there and died.

She knew she couldn't leave the body here, but she couldn't stay either. Why couldn't she stay? Well, because she needed to keep driving just in case Brad was out there looking for her. She couldn't let him find her. It would be too easy to dispose of her body out here, especially since there were no witnesses around. Nothing but woods.

Maybe she should try to get the body into the car and find help instead of sitting here doing nothing but wasting the precious time and gas she had left. Then, another thought popped into her head. What if she got pulled over while having the body in the backseat? What would she tell the police officer? Well, she'd tell them the truth: that she had found the body in the middle of the road and didn't want to leave it there. She would explain that she tried to call for help but had no service—no bars because she was in the woods, and the trees were blocking the towers. All she wanted to do was find help. But would they believe her? She wasn't from this town; they'd think she had killed this person, hit them, and would bury the body somewhere.

"Bury the body," she mumbled. "Come on, Sara!" Her mind was spinning in circles, like a hurricane forming in the ocean. She had done nothing wrong! She was driving by and saw this person. She wanted to help. That was it. End of story! She hadn't killed them, hadn't run them over with her car. Had she?

"No!" she shouted.

Her body was exhausted, while her mind fabricated scenarios that made her think and believe she had done this, even though she had just arrived. She hadn't killed this person. All she knew was that she couldn't leave the body. Period!

"Fine," she muttered. She zipped up her coat and flipped up the hood, snapping it into place so the wind wouldn't blow it off. She would get soaked, but that was the least of her worries.

It was now or never.

She thrust open the door and planted both feet on the pavement. She gripped the handle and pulled herself up and out of the car just as a gust of wind hit her, throwing her back inside. She lost her grip on the door handle, and the door slammed against her knees, causing her back to strike the steering wheel. A sharp, electrifying bolt of pain shot through her body. To top it off, her teeth bit into her bottom lip. She tasted blood.

"Son of a monkey's ass," she swore, licking the metallic, coppery taste from her lower lip.

She grabbed the steering wheel with one hand and the outer frame of the car with the other, hoisting herself up. She moved to the side and slammed the car door behind her before Mother Nature could get any other ideas.

The wind pushed against her, causing her to stumble sideways, like a two-step in a line dance—*step to the left. Cross over to the right. Turn in a circle and kick your right foot out, and then your left.*

She grounded her feet in place and stood tall. Now all she needed to do was move forward and walk to the body in the road. But she couldn't move as her eyes fell to the person's face, locking eyes with them. Sara could have sworn she saw the person blink, but it could have been the rain hazing her vision, making her think the eyes had moved. Or maybe she had blinked.

She took a step closer, battling the wind and rain as if Mother Nature didn't want her to assist this person. She knelt as the wind tried to blow her over, pressing her knees firmly to the ground. Small pebbles dug into the bone of her kneecap.

She wasn't sure she could withstand any more pain tonight. She lifted each knee and brushed away the small rocks. Her back was still spasming, and she was certain a bruise had already formed where she had hit the steering wheel.

She stared at the face for a moment longer before reaching out and placing two fingers on the side of their neck.

"Oh shit," she gasped.

There was a pulse.

Chapter 3

The person was still alive, her head repeated. She had to do something—now! She couldn't leave the person here if they were alive. *But you were going to,* her mind reminded her.

"They're alive," she whispered.

Light shot across the sky, giving her a moment to see the person's face. Sara was certain that it was a woman—a female.

Sara shifted her gaze from the girl's face to her body. Before the light in the sky disappeared, Sara noticed that the coat was pink.

"Definitely a girl," Sara mumbled.

The girl was wearing a pair of Vans that Sara was sure had once been white, but now looked darker, possibly coated with mud. Had the girl come running out of the woods in the pouring rain and been hit by an oncoming car? A car that hadn't seen her struck her and left the scene? Or had the person driving the vehicle believed that it was a deer and continued on, thinking nothing of it? Why had Sara assumed that a car had hit the girl at all? Sure, it was possible that the girl had reached the road and collapsed, hoping someone would find her, just as Sara had.

Perhaps it was the same reason Sara was running away. All Sara knew was that she couldn't leave the poor girl out here. She needed to get her in the car and find help.

"Yes, help. I need to find help," Sara repeated, as if she

were trying to convince herself of this. After all, there was no one else here but her and this poor, helpless girl.

Sara looked back at the car, which had only two doors. She would need to fold the seat forward and carefully lay the girl in the backseat. Then she remembered her leg and glanced in that direction. It was twisted, but she couldn't tell in the dark if it had broken the skin.

Another thing she didn't notice was blood. If there had been blood, the rain would have washed it all away. The rain would have removed all the evidence from the accident. But again, Sara didn't know if there had been an accident—a hit and run, as most people called it. Which, in her eyes, it had been. It was the only explanation.

Sara stood; her knee-high boots felt heavy, as if filled with cement, making it hard to move. She was anchored to the spot, with the wind trying to knock her over like a bowling pin. She pushed her way back through the wind and rain toward the car. She opened the driver's side door, pulled the lever on the back of the driver's seat up, and folded the seat forward against the steering wheel.

Thunder boomed and lightning shot across the sky. Sara tossed her luggage over the front seat and spread the blanket onto the backseat. She couldn't take the chance of ruining the interior with rainwater. This was authentic leather, and, on top of that, it was white. What would happen if blood got on it? Her grandmother would surely kill her if she did anything to destroy the value of this car.

Yes, I couldn't let that happen, Sara thought, shaking her head. Her grandmother would understand that she was only trying to save a life, that Sara had done a good deed, and her grandmother would forgive her for soiling the seats with blood and rainwater.

Once she finished laying the thick blanket across the seat—a blanket her grandmother had said to leave in the car just in case something terrible happened and she needed to stay warm—she stepped out of the car and stood.

The rain had finally let up, and the wind had died down. Had Mother Nature been watching her this whole time and sparing her a few minutes to get the girl in the car before letting it pour down on her again? Maybe, but Sara doubted this was true.

She didn't have that kind of luck. Not lately, anyway. The past year had been a total waste of her life. Well, since she had said yes to Brad. Not that she had known he was an abusive and controlling person, or that he had anger issues, which he seemed to take out on her. She should have known there was something wrong with him, as she hadn't seen him with a girlfriend ever. First, check past relationships; if he had never dated before, then run away. Second, if he yells at you for any reason, run away.

But her excuse will always be that she was just too young to know any better. She was a teenager, and girls her age think they know what true love is and that the first guy who tells them that he loves them is the one they will marry, and they will live happily ever after.

WRONG!

She had been too naïve and stuck in the dream stage of what every girl believed love was until she saw the truth for herself. Sure, it took her a couple of beatings before she got smart and realized that Brad wasn't ever going to change, that he would not stop hitting her. He had issues, and he needed help. This she had told him, and she paid for the words that had left her tongue. Brad had been furious that she would even consider him having any flaws at all.

Sara wiped the tear from her cheek. She hadn't realized that she had been crying as her mind thought of Brad. Though she didn't believe that they were tears of sadness. No, she knew that she was crying because she had been so wrong about him, and now look at her. She was running away from him because, yes, her life depended on it. But she couldn't think about that now. She had to help this girl and find a hospital.

Sara took a deep breath, exhaled, and turned around.

Chapter 4

The road was empty. There was no one in the middle of the road. Had Sara fabricated the whole thing? Had none of it been real?

"No! No, freaking way did I just make all of this up!" she shouted. She felt as if she were losing her mind. Had Brad struck her in the head, so that she was imagining things that weren't really there?

Yes! Yes, that had to be what was happening, she thought. But she knew that wasn't the case. Or at least, she hoped that it wasn't? She didn't know. What she knew was that she needed to check the surrounding area before the storm clouds unleashed again.

Sara didn't move. Instead, she started laughing. She roared so loudly that her voice echoed all around her. She was surely losing it now. The girl had a broken leg. There was no way in hell she could have just stood up and walked or even run into the woods.

Sara stepped forward to the middle of the road, where she was sure she had seen the body. There on the ground was a necklace, a necklace with a half heart hanging from it, featuring the letters **BE** and **FRI**, which meant that someone was wearing the other half with the letters **ST** and **ENDS** on it. Sara had seen a necklace like this before because she had one just like it. Her long-ago best friend, Maria, had given it to her before she left and moved to California with her dad.

Sara picked up the necklace between her fingers. She looked down at the chain lying in her palm and then glanced at the woods in front of her. Now that the rain had stopped, she could hear any movement in the forest. If the girl took off into the woods, Sara would hear her running, but she truly doubted that the girl was running. There was no way, not after seeing her leg twisted to the side.

Sara walked to the other side of the road and looked down into the ditch, but she saw nothing. She looked further down to the left and then to the right. Nothing. It was too dark to see anything. But where did the girl go? This question she couldn't answer.

Sara stared into the woods ahead and leaned forward as if it would help her see or hear better. Nothing. She didn't even hear an animal make a sound, though she doubted animals would be out in a storm. Well, she knew she wouldn't go trudging through the woods looking for someone she didn't know; someone who didn't want her help. Because if they did, they wouldn't have run from her. She hadn't imagined the girl, had she?

She looked back down at her hand; the necklace was still there, but that didn't mean it hadn't been on the road long before she stopped here. The chain wasn't rusted, as she was sure it would be if it had been lying here for more than a few days, especially with all the crazy weather they'd been having. The salt would surely make the necklace rust or change color, like green or something, wouldn't it? And if it had been snowing, like it should be in November rather than being fifty degrees, she wouldn't be having this dilemma because she would see tracks in the snow, but it wasn't snowing.

Sara heard the raindrop hit the hood of her coat and looked up at the sky. It was too dark to see any clouds, and there were definitely no stars out, but she was sure they were somewhere above the dark clouds.

Another drop splattered onto her face, then another. She turned around and hurried back to the car just as the sky opened and rain pelted down. She opened the car door, pushed back the driver's seat, and jumped inside, slamming the door shut. She removed the hood from her head and ran a hand through her long blonde hair. Before putting the car in drive, she looked back out the window to her left and saw nothing but darkness. She wouldn't be telling anyone about tonight; besides, who would believe her anyway? She had no evidence except this necklace in her hand.

She repaired the broken clasp and hung the necklace over the rearview mirror. The half-heart glistened in the light from the dashboard. Sara shifted into drive and pulled back onto the road, heading further into the town of Craven Falls.

As she drove, she kept a lookout for the girl but was sure she wouldn't see her. Sara was only trying to help her. Why would the girl run from her? Sara was certain she had made the whole thing up because of the tragic state of her mind. One's state of mind can make you see things that aren't there. This was something she had learned in psychology. She had been fleeing to get as far away from Brad as possible. She was tired and confused. She probably imagined the entire thing.

The further she drove, the more she accepted that what she had seen was a figment of her imagination. That it wasn't real. She couldn't allow what she had thought she saw to be real. No one just disappears into thin air, but the girl had, and that's why Sara needed to drop the whole thing and forget about it. Besides, she had her own life to worry about.

But she couldn't let this go. Her eyes moved to the necklace hanging down. As much as she wanted to, she had to believe what she had seen. She placed two fingers on the girl's neck and felt a pulse.

Up ahead, Sara spotted a building in the distance, followed by another. She had finally arrived in the town of Craven Falls. Though it appeared lifeless, it was the middle of the night. Stores were closed and people were asleep, so naturally, there would be no lights on inside the buildings or houses.

As she drove through the sleepy town, she saw a sign up ahead: **Falls Bed and Breakfast**. Excitement swept over her, and she decided to stay for the night and leave the following day after resting her weary body.

She pulled her car alongside the road and shifted into park. She looked out the passenger window and up at the Victorian house that reminded her of the trip she had taken with her grandmother years ago to Maine, where she had seen Stephen King's house.

Maybe she thought she was in Maine, but she knew she wasn't. Although the town looked like a Castle Rock setting, the body in the road, coupled with being in this town, sure felt like one of his mastermind horror books.

Sara turned off the car and grabbed her suitcase from the front seat. She opened the car door, stepped out, and hurried up the sidewalk to the front door. She felt bad about knocking on the front door and waking the owner of this Bed and Breakfast, but what else could she do? She didn't want to sleep in her car; she wanted a nice, warm bed to sink into and sleep until her body felt rested.

She climbed the wooden steps and stood under the porch eave. She hesitated for two seconds before reaching out her hand to press the doorbell. She listened as the sound of the doorbell echoed through the house.

Chapter 5

Minutes later, Sara noticed a light flickering on in the window to her right, followed by the sound of shuffling feet across what seemed like wooden floors. Someone was approaching the door. Sara straightened up, but she felt the tension ball up in her shoulders once again.

She had no idea whether the person behind the door would be angry at her for ringing the doorbell at such a late hour. Usually, if someone were mad, they would mumble and swear at the person upsetting them, but she heard nothing but the sound of padded feet making their way to the front door. She tried to relax her shoulders, but it was already too late for that. Once she became stressed, the muscles in her shoulders and neck would remain tense for hours.

The deadbolt clicked, and then the knob turned. The door swung open with a *swoosh,* and light flooded in, causing Sara to close her eyes and reopen them to adjust to the brightness that had momentarily blinded her. When she opened her eyes, she saw a little old woman standing in the doorway. The woman stood at least half a foot shorter than Sara and wore a heavy, soft pink cotton robe fastened in a half bow around her thin waist. The color reminded Sara of the pink coat the girl had worn earlier, but then again, had she really seen the coat?

Sara smiled at the woman who had opened the door. The woman had dark circles under her eyes and appeared just as dog-tired as Sara felt. In fact, Sara was beyond exhausted and surprised she was still standing there without having collapsed from fatigue. Her feet felt heavy and achy in her boots. Neither of them spoke a word as they stood there, both half-asleep in the entryway.

The old woman tried to straighten, but Sara could tell that she had a rounded back. She knew what that meant as her grandmother had the same hump caused by Osteoporosis because of increased bone weakness, making the back curve and no longer straight.

The old woman lifted her head, blinked tiredly, and looked at Sara. Her eyes were a shade of blue, like the sky on a bright sunny day, just like the skies she remembered seeing in Florida when she vacationed with her mom.

"Hi, I'm sorry to be bothering you this late, but I'm looking for a place to rest for the night," Sara said. "I didn't see any motel in town, just this Bed and Breakfast." She stopped talking and waited for the woman to speak, but she didn't say a word. The old woman simply stepped aside for Sara to enter.

Sara stepped through the threshold, and the door closed with a heavy *thud* behind her. The deadbolt *clicked* back into place as if the woman were afraid someone might come in while they stood there. The old woman had good reason to be afraid. How would she protect herself with such a fragile body?

Sara turned and glanced down at the woman. "Again, I'm so sorry to have bothered you," she repeated.

"Nonsense," the woman finally replied in a wheezy voice and then coughed into her hand. "I don't get many visitors here, especially at night." The woman strained to look into Sara's eyes. "But you don't seem like a person who might hurt an old lady like me."

Sara seemed a little surprised by the words. "Oh, no. Certainly not," Sara replied, feeling distraught by the old woman's words. How could someone think she would hurt anyone? But then again, this woman didn't know her, did she?

"Follow me, I'll show you to your room for the night."

Sara followed the woman up the dark oak staircase. She was sure she might age another year before they reached the top. Though she had to be patient since she was in this woman's house.

The old woman rested at the top of the landing, catching her breath before moving further down the hallway. She stopped at the second door on the right, opened the bedroom door, and flicked on the light.

Sara moved around the woman and into the room, where she saw an elegant cherry canopy bed adorned with a sheer white scarf draped over the top and cascading down the sides. The bedding, also white, featured flowers embroidered with matching pillow shams. It was the most gorgeous bed Sara had ever seen.

"Will this room suit you for the night?" the old woman inquired.

Sara was speechless. The room was immaculate and more beautiful than any bedroom she had seen in all her seventeen years.

"It's perfect," Sara finally stated.

"Wonderful. The bathroom is down the hall for you to clean up, and since it's late, I'll wait to cook you something after you wake up."

Sara nodded and turned to look at the woman. "Thank

you so much for allowing me to stay here."

"My pleasure. Get some rest," the woman said, and padded off down the hall, making her way back downstairs, where Sara believed the woman slept.

Sara closed the bedroom door and placed her suitcase on one of those luggage stands seen in hotels. *What were they called,* she wondered, until the word she sought came to her? Lancaster table. Yes, because this was something else her grandmother had referenced long ago in one of her many stories, which was not important at this moment.

She gazed around the room, absorbing every detail from the carved walnut trim along the floor and ceiling to the furniture scattered throughout. She felt a bit sad that she would be leaving in the morning, but did she have to? She couldn't think about that now. First, she would get undressed, crawl under those blankets, and figure out what to do in the morning.

Chapter 6

Morning light filtered through the white satin curtains that hung across the long rectangular windows in the bedroom where Sara was sleeping. She lay under the quilted white blanket, still fast asleep, dreaming of nothing. Her body, exhausted from the night before, had fallen into a deep, unfamiliar slumber—a sleep she hadn't experienced in a long time.

As the early morning hours passed and afternoon made its appearance, Sara opened her bluish-gray eyes. Her slim, five-foot-six figure felt relaxed and rested. She placed her arms above her head, giving her muscles and bones a much-needed waking stretch. She hadn't felt this good in a long time. In fact, she couldn't recall the last time she had slept so sound—so deep.

She hoped that Brad wouldn't find her here, but she also wasn't sure if she was staying or just passing through. Aside from the Bed and Breakfast, she had no idea what this town looked like or what kinds of people lived here. It wasn't as though she had a ton of cash on her to rent this room for more than a few days. Hell, she didn't even know how much it cost to stay here. A place this nice had to cost a few hundred dollars a night, and that would use up half of her cash.

Sara slipped out from under the warmth of the blankets that had enveloped her. She wore a pair of grey cotton shorts and a thin t-shirt, which she was sure were not appropriate for a place like this. Running a hand through her tangled mess of hair, she wondered if she had been tossing and turning last night. She didn't remember having any nightmares, which she seemed to experience most nights when she slept.

She placed her bare feet on the floor, which felt as cold as ice. She hadn't thought to bring a pair of slippers for her feet. She stood, looking down beside the nightstand, and saw a pair of ladies' slippers. Had they been there last night? She wasn't sure and decided not to dwell on it. She slipped her feet into the slippers and padded toward the door.

Then it hit her. What if there were other guests staying here? She turned away from the door and walked over to what she hoped was a closet. She opened it, and there, in front of her, on a hanger, was a long, white cotton robe. She grabbed the robe off the hanger and slipped her arms through the openings, wrapping the soft fabric around her bare skin.

The hallway was empty as she stepped into it. She glanced around at all the doors, searching for the bathroom, hoping it was unoccupied. She hurried down the hall to the only open door she saw. She flicked on the light, noticed a sink, toilet, and a clawfoot tub, and closed the bathroom door.

* * *

An hour later, Sara made her way downstairs. She had showered and changed into a clean pair of clothes, leaving her suitcase in the room since she wasn't sure what she would be doing: whether to stay or leave.

As she descended the wooden staircase, she gazed around at the rooms below. The place appeared flawless. A grandfather clock stood against the wall, and she noticed that it was past noon. She hadn't slept this late in a long time. Her grandmother was ill, and Sara would get up early to help care for her.

Sara's mother had left when Sara was ten, leaving her in her grandmother's care, and moved to Florida. As for her father, well, she didn't know where he was. He had left before she was even born, and her mother didn't like to talk about him, so she didn't ask questions. She just hoped that her grandmother would forgive her for leaving the way she had and taking her precious car with her. Maybe she would call her later to let her know that she was fine, that the car was fine, but not to tell anyone that she had called. But then her grandmother would ask questions—questions Sara wasn't ready to answer.

She stepped off the last step and stood in the open foyer. Light beamed in through the stained-glass windows that surrounded the room, giving her a chance to see everything she hadn't noticed when she arrived last night. She wondered if the old lady had someone to help her clean the house. She was sure that she did because the place was too big for the old woman to handle by herself.

Sara walked into the room to her left. There were two burgundy sofas and a matching chair, separated by end tables. Built into the wall was an elegant fireplace with a cherry mantle that displayed cherished family photos.

There was no fire burning in the fireplace, not that the room needed one, as it was already warm enough. Besides, she was sure they had updated the place with a heating system. She knew fireplaces weren't just for heating a house; they provided a cozy feeling. She imagined herself sitting on the sofa, reading a book while the logs crackled and hissed.

She stepped further into the room and studied the paintings on the wall. There were knick-knacks of every kind, mostly ceramic birds. This reminded her of her grandmother, who also had ceramic birds in a wooden curio cabinet in the dining room back home in Bristol. Was this something that older women liked to collect?

"Ah, I see that you are up. Can I get you something to eat?" asked the old woman.

Sara jumped at the unexpected voice that filled the room. She placed a hand on her breast and turned toward the woman, her heart pounding in her chest.

"Oh, I'm sorry to have scared you," the woman said. "I get scared a lot these days, too."

"Sorry, you just caught me off guard. I rarely scare that easily," Sara lied. Ever since she had seen what Brad did, she was more frightened now than ever.

"Come, I'll make you something to eat."

Sara followed the old lady past the open foyer and into the kitchen. Sara's eyes skimmed over the dark, green-painted cabinets that hung around the room. The counter was cluttered with small appliances, including a blender, two toasters, an old antique mixer, a wooden chopping board, and several vases of flowers, leaving little space for any activity. Her eyes drifted around the room, traveling to the other side where she spotted a rectangular walnut table with eight chairs tucked neatly underneath it.

Instead of sitting at the table alone, since there seemed to be no other guests in the house, Sara pulled out a bar stool and sat on the other side of the center island. She watched as the elderly woman opened the fridge and began taking out food, but then paused and looked at Sara.

"Oh, please forgive my forgetfulness. I didn't ask you what you wanted to eat, my dear?"

Sara smiled, "Whatever you have is fine. You don't need to go to any trouble to feed me."

"Nonsense, it wouldn't be a Bed and Breakfast if I didn't cook for you. I'm here to serve you," the kind lady replied.

Sara wasn't sure what to say to that, but she felt guilty for letting this old lady take care of her. She stood and walked around the counter. "How about you sit down, and I make myself something to eat? I'm sure you could use some pampering yourself," Sara said.

The woman laughed at this, as though she had received a compliment.

"I didn't catch your name when I arrived here last night," Sara said.

"Oh, yes, it was late, and my mind doesn't think like it used to," the woman said as she sat down at the walnut table. "My name is Edith Blackstone, some people here in Craven Falls just call me Ed for short, although to me it sounds like a man's name, but I don't make a fuss. I know they're talking to me." Edith nodded.

"Well, it's nice to meet you, Edith, my name is Sara." She wondered for a split second if she should have given Edith a false name, but she was sure the woman wouldn't go to the police. Sara had done nothing wrong or given Edith a reason to turn her in. As far as the old lady knew, Sara was just passing through town and needed a place to stay for the night.

"So, what is there to do in this town for fun?" Sara asked, trying to make conversation.

"Fun?" Edith seemed to question. "Well, I don't know if there is anything *fun* to do here. It's ***mostly*** just a quiet town. Everyone here knows everyone. We keep to ourselves. Well, I do, at least," Edith laughed. "I don't know about the others; besides, I don't get out as much as I used to. I have friends who bring me what I need from the store."

Sara nodded, even though she was sure she didn't agree with Edith. What was there to do in a town devoid of activities? It seemed dull to her, but maybe it was exactly what she needed.

"How old are you?" asked Edith. "You look young. I was young once, you know. But," Edith laughed again, "that was eons ago. Can't remember much of my youth these days. My mind seems to slip away from me. I'm lucky to wake up every morning. God must think there's a reason for me to keep on living, you know." Edith frowned at this. "My husband Fred died six years ago, and it's just been me in this house, all alone."

Sara felt a pang in her chest. The old lady had to live here alone. She was lonely; who wouldn't be? Though the woman had said she was all alone, not lonely. Wasn't there a difference?

And should she lie to Edith about her age? She didn't feel right lying to this kind woman, an old woman who had allowed Sara into her home in the middle of the night. But she felt no reason to lie to Edith and was sad that the old lady had no one here to help her.

Silence filled the air around them as neither woman spoke. Sara hoped that Edith would forget she had asked how old she was, but she didn't—Edith asked again. This time, Sara replied.

"I'm seventeen, going to be eighteen next week," Sara lied again. She didn't have to tell her the whole truth—the truth that she wasn't turning eighteen until the following August, which was nine months away.

"Have you finished school?"

Sara shook her head as she opened the cabinet door, searching for a plate.

"Next door over," Edith said, as if she could read Sara's mind.

Sara opened the adjacent cabinet door and took out a plate.

"Do you want something to eat?" asked Sara.

"No, I ate several hours ago. I don't eat much these days. Now that I'm in my mid-eighties, eating doesn't seem as important."

Sara knew that this was true. Her grandmother only ate twice a day, at most. Mostly, she nibbled on food throughout the day.

There's a high school here if you're looking to finish school. Are you a senior?

"Oh, ah, yeah. I have one year left of high school." Sara wasn't sure where this conversation was going, as she barely knew this kind old woman.

"If you're looking for a place to stay, you're more than welcome to live here and finish school. I would love to have you here," Edith said before continuing. "It would be nice to have someone in this house with me. You wouldn't be a bother."

Sara stiffened as she held the lettuce in her hand. Without moving her head, she looked over at Edith, who, thank God, wasn't watching her. She swallowed and finished placing the lettuce and tomatoes on the sandwich. Did this woman know who Sara was and why she was on the run?

Chapter 7

After she ate, Sara explored the rest of the town. Part of her considered staying here and accepting Edith's offer, but it felt wrong to her. She worried she would be taking advantage of Edith by living here for free. Not that she thought she wouldn't have to pay for her stay, or possibly work at the Bed and Breakfast to cover her expenses. It would be a perfect place for her to stay until she returned home, if she ever went home at all.

Sara walked down Washington Street, which seemed to be the main road running through the small town. She passed several homes and noticed that they were all different, not the same Victorian style in which Edith lived. She wasn't sure why she had assumed that a town like this would have houses that all looked alike.

She strolled by a grocery store that she was sure carried the essential items people needed so they didn't have to make a long drive out of town for bread, eggs, and milk. She saw a café across the street that, through the glass window, seemed busy with customers. She didn't recall seeing a sign indicating the population in this town, nor did it really matter, but she was sure that it wasn't many. Even the town of Bristol, from which she had come, didn't have a large number of people living in it.

She continued walking, not that there was much else to see or do here, because once she crossed over Breacher and Kale, there appeared to be nothing but land and trees. The houses seemed to grow further apart.

In the distance, she saw a long building and several bleachers, which she was sure was the high school that Edith had told her about. Should she take a walk there to check it out? Maybe see if it was a place she'd like to attend? She heard a sound and turned toward the woods to her right. She saw nothing that caught her eye. *It was probably an animal rooting around in the leaves and branches that lined the forest,* she thought.

She turned around, but not before noticing something much farther into the woods. It was something she nearly missed but caught her eye at the last second.

Something pink.

Her heart raced as her mind replayed last night's events and the body she saw on the road. She was sure she had seen the girl, but then she had vanished into thin air.

She stood and traced over the wooded area. Should she go into the woods and see if the girl in the pink coat was there? She might need help. *Yes, of course, she would need help.* She reminded herself that she had a broken leg. How had the girl walked with the bone protruding through the skin, but Sara wasn't certain that the bone was sticking outside the flesh because she wasn't sure what she had seen. She was certain there wasn't any blood on the road. But the rain could have washed it away. If the bone snapped in half and had broken through the skin, there was no way in hell this girl could walk. The girl would have been in excruciating pain, wouldn't she?

Well, Sara knew she had two choices. One, check out the woods and see if she had really seen the girl in the pink coat. Or two, turn around and walk back to the Bed and Breakfast and forget what she had seen last night or thought she had seen seconds ago. That her mind had fabricated the whole scene in her head from exhaustion and fear.

But she couldn't stand here and do nothing; that was for sure. Sara wasn't someone who could walk away, but hadn't she done just that? She had stolen her grandmother's car and driven like a bat out of hell, ending up here in Craven Falls. She knew she needed to go into the woods just to make sure, to ensure that there wasn't someone who needed help. Her help.

Sara stepped off the sidewalk and into the woods. Her boot sank half an inch into the soggy ground. She had forgotten all about the rain that soaked the earth last night. The sun dried the road, but not the forest.

She headed in the direction she believed she had seen the pink coat. Branches snapped beneath her knee-high boots, the same boots she had worn last night. In fact, they were the only shoes she owned because she hadn't thought to grab another pair. All that occupied her mind was getting the heck away from Brad.

She turned around to see how far she had gone from the road. Twenty, thirty feet. She didn't know because, to be honest, she wasn't good at math. Numbers just weren't her thing. Now, cooking—that was her thing.

She stood and glanced around, listening to the noises all around her. Birds chirped and sang as streams of sunlight poked through the tree branches. Although she couldn't see the birds, she could hear their conversations and wondered, for a second, what they were talking about. She laughed at herself for thinking about something so strange, but she was sure that she wasn't the only person in the world who might have thought the same thing and had the same questions.

She took three steps forward and crashed to the ground. Her hand sank into the mud and moldy, wet leaves before her knee connected with the earth. She glanced over her shoulder and saw that her foot had plunged into a hole, twisting her ankle. She allowed herself to lie there on her side for a moment before turning over and sitting up. She pulled her foot out of the hole and brushed her hands off on her jeans, which had gotten dirty from the fall.

"Shit," she swore. "This is just freaking great!" Her words echoed around her.

"Are you okay?" a girl with long, black, wavy hair asked, standing on the edge of the road just outside the wood line.

Sara wasn't sure how long the girl had been standing there. She had been facing the other way until she fell to the ground.

She planted her hands on the ground beside her and tried to push herself up, but the moment she put weight on her foot, the pain in her ankle forced her back down onto the branches and pine needles covering the earth beneath her.

"Here, let me help you." The girl who had just asked if she was okay appeared out of nowhere and put her arm around Sara, helping her up.

Sara held her right foot off the ground and stood with the support of this girl. How had the girl reached her so quickly? Did it matter? Not really.

"Thank you," Sara said.

"Sure, it's no problem. My name is Mickey, but my friends call me Mick for short." She stated. "You're not from around here, are you?"

"No, I just drove into town last night. Just passing

through."

"Oh? Where are you staying?"

This Mick girl was filled with questions, and Sara wasn't sure if she should tell her anything. She decided to keep it simple: no details.

"At the Bed and Breakfast."

"Edith?"

Sara nodded.

"What were you doing in here anyway?" Mick asked, glancing around.

Sara shifted her eyes toward the ground where the hole was. "I thought I saw something and wanted to check it out, but then I fell into that hole."

Mick appeared to nod in agreement. "Here, let me help you back to Edith's place."

"Thanks," Sara replied. "But you don't have to. I can manage."

"I don't think so," Mick stated.

Mick seemed to be right about Sara not being able to walk on her own because once they were out of the woods, she put weight on her ankle. The pain was worse than before, and she prayed that she hadn't broken her foot, which meant she wouldn't be leaving this town today or anytime soon. But mostly, she didn't want to go to the hospital because she was sure that the doctor would call her grandmother, and then she would have to go back home.

As soon as they both climbed the stairs of the Bed and Breakfast, the door swung open.

Edith asked, her eyebrows creased, "Are you alright, my dear?"

"She fell in the woods down the street and hurt her foot,"

Mick replied.

"In the woods?" Edith questioned. "What in God's name were you doing in the woods?"

I asked her that same question myself. She said she thought she saw something.

"Well, come in, come in. We'll need to get her foot up and look at it," Edith said.

Mick assisted Sara into the house and to the sofa, while Edith headed into the kitchen to fetch some ice.

"Thank you so much for your help," Sara said.

"I didn't catch your name?" Mick seemed to ask instead of accepting the compliment.

That's because I didn't give it to you, Sara thought. "Sara."

"Well, nice to meet you, Sara. Although I wish it were under different circumstances," Mick said, then glanced at the clock on the wall. "Oh, no, I'm late. Sorry to have to leave so soon, but I need to get to the café for my shift."

Sara nodded as Mick practically dashed to the door, shouting to Edith that she needed to go.

Edith entered the room just as the front door closed. "That girl is always in a hurry," Edith said.

Sara unzipped her boot, slid her foot out, and laid it on the pillow Mick had placed there before she left. She pulled her pant leg up and removed her sock. Her ankle didn't appear broken, just slightly swollen.

Edith handed her the ice pack, and Sara gently placed it on her ankle. She flinched at the coldness of the ice against her skin.

"You rest here, and I'll start a fire," Edith said.

"Oh, you don't need to do that," Sara replied.

"Well, I don't think you'll be doing much else today, so why not start a fire and relax a bit?"

Sara nodded at this because she wasn't going to disagree with Edith, who appeared capable of winning almost any argument.

"After everything that has happened lately in this town, I'm surprised half the people still live here, but no one seems to care," Edith muttered, as if talking to herself.

Sara wasn't sure if she should ask what Edith meant by that and decided she'd leave it for another time. Perhaps a question to consider for later when they needed something to discuss.

Ten minutes later, with the soothing sound of the fire hissing and crackling, Sara slowly drifted off to sleep, her mind focused solely on the girl in the pink coat. She felt the need to learn more and decided to stay because she sensed that something was wrong; she didn't know what it was. Besides, she couldn't drive with a hurt ankle.

Chapter 8

Sara woke with a start, her eyes springing open when she heard a knock at the front door. No, not a knock. Someone was pounding on the door, and her first thought was that Brad had found her. He had followed her to this town, and he would kill her; this she was sure of. But then she realized that if it were Brad, why would he be making so much noise? She was jumping to conclusions because she had seen no one following her last night. There were no other headlights behind her. Besides, if Brad had followed her, she wouldn't be here right now. He would have taken her the moment she stepped out of the car to see the body in the road, or when she had gone for a walk earlier.

She closed her eyes, letting her heart settle, and took small, shallow breaths before opening her eyes again. It was quiet, except for the sound of the fire crackling as she stared up at the ceiling. Maybe she had dreamt the whole thing, and there was no one at the door.

Yes, she had fallen asleep shortly after Edith started the fire. The heat and sound from the flames made Sara feel drowsy. She pushed herself up to a sitting position on the sofa. The events of the day rushed back to her as she looked at her foot propped up on the pillow. She had fallen and injured her ankle.

The knock on the door sounded again, this time somewhat louder. Sara didn't see Edith anywhere and assumed she had either gone out or was napping in another room. Or perhaps it was Edith knocking on the door; maybe she had locked herself out.

Sara placed both feet on the Persian rug covering the wooden floor in the family room and applied weight to her twisted ankle. The pain wasn't as terrible or excruciating as it had been earlier.

She hobbled toward the door, hoping to open it before the person knocked again. She turned the deadbolt and pulled on the door, but it didn't budge. She leaned forward, putting weight on her good foot, and yanked the door toward her, losing her balance. She placed her free hand on the doorframe to prevent herself from falling.

"Oh, good, you're up," Mick said, standing on the porch.

Sara hadn't noticed how pretty Mick's smile was, but that could be because Mick hadn't smiled until now. *Her mind raced back to earlier when Mick had appeared beside her in the woods. Sara had paid little attention to the girl's face at the time. After all, she was more focused on what she thought she saw in the woods—or what she believed she saw, because she had seen nothing at all. All Sara knew was that she had only met this girl twice, and she seemed excessively happy, if that were a thing.* Sara slipped out of her thoughts and nodded before moving aside to let Mick in.

"I hope I'm not bothering you. I thought for sure Edith would answer the door. I didn't mean for you to get up and answer the door. I'm so sorry. How's the foot?"

"It's no problem, really," Sara replied. She could tell that Mick's emotions had switched from happy to concerned, or maybe this was how the girl always acted; she wasn't sure. She hadn't planned on making any friends while she was here. And yet, here she was, making friends. Could she even call Mick a friend?

Sara ambled back to the sofa and placed her foot on the pillow.

Mick took a seat across from Sara, closer to the fireplace, and rubbed her hands together as if trying to ignite a spark. "So, are you feeling better?" Mick asked.

Sara nodded. "Yeah, not as much pain as earlier."

"Looks like the swelling went down, too."

How could Mick know if the swelling had gone down if Sara hadn't taken her boot off until Mick had left for work? She was sure she didn't have superpowers to see through Sara's boot.

Mick asked, "So, how long are you staying here?"

Since twisting her ankle, Sara hadn't thought that far ahead. She wasn't even sure she could drive with her foot in its current state. She would probably need a day or two of rest before getting back on the road, heading nowhere in particular. Sara hadn't realized that Mick was still talking when her mind drifted off, contemplating what she would do from here.

"Are you listening? Lots of my friends seem like they're listening, but then they tune me out as if I'm not talking at all. You're not tuning me out, are you?"

"What, no," Sara replied, but she had no idea what Mick had just said to her.

"Because if you didn't hear me, I'll just repeat it," Mick laughed at herself. "God, I talk too much. Tell me I talk too much."

"You talk too much," Sara replied, then laughed. She didn't want to hurt the girl's feelings after just meeting her. "It's fine. Why do you ask so many questions, anyway?"

Mick roared with laughter. "I got it from my mom. I swear, wherever we went, she was always asking a million questions. By the time she finished talking, she had forgotten what she was trying to find out."

Sara nodded as if she agreed with Mick, or maybe she just nodded to feel good about herself; either way, it didn't matter as long as she stopped asking **so many questions**. Sara felt like she was being interrogated by the FBI or CIA, which she was sure Mick was not.

"So, how old are you? You don't look much older than me. I'm seventeen. I turn eighteen in March." Mick smiled.

"Seventeen," Sara said, not adding that she would be eighteen in nine months, even though she had told Edith the next week.

"Did you finish high school early?"

Sara wondered what had happened to her efforts to keep herself hidden. Why had she come to the town of Craven Falls when she wasn't an adult yet? Although no one was asking her those questions, at least not yet. She was sure that Mick would get to that question sooner rather than later.

"No, I'm a senior at my old school."

"You should come to my school. I can introduce you to Rachel and Laura. They would love you," Mick smiled, showing her pearly whites once more.

"I don't know. I don't have a place to stay while I'm here," Sara replied.

"You can stay here. I'm sure Edith wouldn't mind. She could use the company. She hasn't had anyone living with her for six years. Poor Fred. We all miss him. He was such a great guy. Helping when he could," Mick said and then continued. "He used to own the grocery store here in town, and then Edith sold it to Mr. Waters. Mr. Waters also owns the hardware store here in town and Falls Café. If you need a job, I can certainly help you with that."

Sara's mind was spinning, unsure of what Mick was rambling about. Edith, Fred, Mr. Waters? Did this girl ever stop? Did she ever take a breath between words?

"I'll have to think about it," Sara replied, unsure which question she should answer first.

"Well, okay," Mick said, sounding sad at Sara's reply. "It will be Thanksgiving break here, so you have time to decide what you want to do in the next few days."

Chapter 9

The house was silent once again, and Sara felt calm from this. She had never met anyone like Mick before. She was a very enthusiastic girl, that was for sure. That girl could talk a mile a minute, and Sara wondered if they had diagnosed her with ADHD, and if she were, she wasn't on any medication for it.

Sara laughed at this while sitting on the bed in the room where she had slept the previous night. She couldn't get over the day she had. Edith had invited Mick to stay for dinner, but Sara was sure Edith hadn't expected Mick to talk the entire time. Edith had to reheat Mick's food because she talked so much that it had gotten cold.

But one thing was for sure: she wanted to investigate the girl she had seen in the pink coat. She knew she hadn't hallucinated—or at least, she didn't want to believe that she had. But where would she start? She was confident she could get all her information from Mick, as the girl was full of facts about this town.

Sara slipped under the warmth of the blankets and stared up at the ceiling. She recalled something Edith had mentioned earlier. It surprised her that people still lived in this town after what had happened here.

The more Sara thought about what Edith had said, the more she wanted to know. But how was she going to find out? She couldn't use her phone to search for information about Craven Falls because she didn't want to risk Brad waiting for her to turn on her phone, at which point he would find her. Then it came to her. She was sure that if there were a high school here, there had to be a library, right?

* * *

The next morning, Sara woke up early. She showered, got dressed, and carefully made her way downstairs to the kitchen, where she found Edith sitting at the table, nursing a cup of coffee.

"Good morning," Sara sang as she entered the room. She couldn't believe how cheerful she was this morning, something she hadn't felt in a long time. Her ankle barely hurt like it did last night.

"Good morning," Edith replied. "Can I get you something to drink or eat?"

"Sit, I can get my coffee, and I'm not hungry just yet, but if I get hungry, I can make it myself," Sara said. "You don't need to wait on me. I can do it."

"Oh, well, thank you, dear, but it's a Bed and Breakfast. I'm supposed to take care of you, not the other way around; besides, what about your foot?"

"I understand, but I'm good," Sara said as she grabbed a cup hanging from a metal holder beside the coffeepot and poured herself a cup. She walked across the room and sat down diagonally from Edith. "My foot is feeling better; I just have to take it slow."

"Have you thought about staying and finishing school?" Edith asked.

Sara let out a soft chuckle at the words Edith had just spoken. "Well, if you don't mind me staying here for a little while. I'm not sure if I will stay and go to school, but I'd like to stay for a day or two at least."

Edith's shoulders drooped in response.

"But I'd like to know what the cost is to rent a room. You haven't asked me for any money."

"No, I guess I haven't."

Sara paused before speaking again, certain that Edith would say something else.

"I'd like for you to stay, but I don't want any money."

"Edith, I can't stay here and not pay you," Sara replied. "I'm eating your food and sleeping in one of your rooms."

"I'm just happy to have someone here. I've been so lonely, you know," Edith frowned at her words.

Sara nodded because she knew that if she spoke, she might cry. No one had ever told her they were happy she was around—something she wished her mother had said at least once in her life. But their conversations were never pleasant, as they continuously fought about something over the phone, though Sara didn't care.

"Well, in that case, I'd love to stay here, but… but if you won't let me pay you, then I will help around the house. I will clean and cook. If you need your laundry done or want to go to the store to get groceries, I'll do it. Does that sound all right with you?" Sara asked.

Edith wiped away a single tear sliding down her thin, wrinkled face and nodded. She reached out and patted Sara's hand resting beside her coffee cup.

Sara's stomach clenched with emotion, and for the first time since her arrival, she felt as if she belonged.

Chapter 10

Since arriving in Craven Falls, Sara hadn't used her car, which was sitting by the curb. She'd ask Edith later, when she returned to the house, if she could park the car in the driveway, out of sight from anyone who might drive by and see her vehicle.

She walked around to the front of the car, opened the door, and climbed inside. The leather seats were freezing, feeling like sharp daggers penetrating the flesh of her butt cheeks through her jeans.

She couldn't believe how quickly the temperatures had dropped since her arrival two days ago. She placed the key in the ignition and turned it, although she was sure the car wouldn't start; instead, the engine came to life with a roar.

While letting the engine warm up, she reached over and opened the glove compartment, taking out her cell phone. She stared at it, contemplating whether she should turn the phone on or toss it back into the glove compartment as if it didn't exist. She didn't want to take any chances of being found. She liked it here in Craven Falls. She wanted it to be her home. She loved living with Edith and talking with Mick, even though Mick seemed to do all the talking.

She turned and looked out the passenger window at the beautiful Victorian house that sat on a small hill. This was her home now, or at least until she decided it was time to move on. Edith wanted her to stay, and this made her feel something she hadn't felt in a very long time, if ever. She felt needed and wanted by this woman who was kind enough to allow her into her home, providing her with a bed and food without charging a dime. In return, Sara would help around the house.

Her mind turned to Brad, whom she had once felt love for, but that hadn't truly been love; she knew that now. She had loved him since she was fourteen, though they hadn't started dating until she was just a little past the age of sixteen. Was that when he finally noticed her? Had he fallen in love with her? This, too, she didn't know. Lately, she seemed *to lack* understanding about many things.

Brad was hard to read. He kept himself closed off regarding emotions. He didn't even show empathy when she was pouring her heart out to him about her mom. He didn't console her when she needed a shoulder to lean on—to cry on. It was as if he didn't care; well, he cared, but only about himself.

"Selfish asshole," she muttered.

It wasn't until the past few months that she saw the real Brad—the one no one else saw. It was as if he was two different people, maybe three if you counted the way he was with his *bro's*, as he called them. He was amazing when they first started dating; she couldn't get enough of him. He was polite, caring, and made her melt every time they were around each other.

Until the past few months.

She believed she was the cause, as he never appeared that way around anyone else. She didn't even know what had prompted him to do what he did.

As for her mother, who was staying at the house while in town, she didn't show Sara any love or indicate that she wanted to be around her. They fought constantly, and Sara was sure that her mother didn't even know she was missing—that she had left days ago, leaving her mom to care for her grandmother. So, what did she have to lose by staying here? *Absolutely nothing,* she thought.

She felt the heat blow out from the heater and placed her hands in front of the vent to warm them. God, it was freezing out here. It was as if she had entered a different region. The weather that had been warm throughout the past two months had changed overnight to a whopping twenty degrees. This shouldn't surprise her, but it did. Living in Ohio, the weather was spontaneous. The winters weren't normally warm, but for some reason, this winter it was. She hadn't dressed for this when she grabbed her things and left. Maybe one day she'd head south and live where it was warmer ninety percent of the time.

"Screw this cold," she murmured, then laughed at herself.

She rubbed her hands together one last time before shifting the car into drive. With the directions Edith had given her that morning, Sara headed straight down Washington Street until she saw the high school come into view, followed by the library. It hadn't taken her more than two minutes to drive here, and she wouldn't have preferred to walk.

She parked next to a black Chevy Impala and looked around, noticing only three other cars in the parking lot besides hers. Had she expected more? *Well, it wasn't like there was much to do here in this town,* she thought.

She climbed the stairs and opened the wooden doors of the library. She stood just inside the doorway, allowing the warmth to console her. She shivered away the cold and embraced the heat blowing down from the vent in the ceiling. She looked around the room. It was smaller than the library back home, which surprised her since Bristol wasn't much bigger in population.

She spotted the counter and walked in that direction. She saw a girl sitting behind the desk, reading a book, which didn't surprise her, as she was in a building full of nothing but books. From where Sara stood, she could see that the girl was around the same age and had soft, wavy brown hair that fell over her shoulders.

The girl looked up as Sara approached the desk. "Hi, you must be the new girl in town. Sara, right?"

Sara felt her eyes widen as she scanned the room to check if anyone else had heard her name. It wasn't that she didn't want anyone to know she was here. She turned back to the girl sitting behind the desk, who had a smile on her face, and nodded in agreement.

"How did you know?" The moment the words left her mouth, she knew the answer, Mick.

"I'm friends with Mick. If you don't want people to know your secrets, then make sure Mick doesn't know them first. She's a lovable person, but not so good at keeping her mouth closed. If you know what I mean," the girl laughed at this, "but I'm sure you know that already. By the way, I'm Laura."

The name Laura seemed familiar to her; then she remembered Mick mentioning that she had a friend named Laura. She sensed that there was something more about her—something relatable between them.

"Hi," Sara smiled.

Laura nodded. "What can I help you with?"

"Do you have any computers that I can use?"

"Yes. Follow me." Laura climbed off the chair and walked around the desk.

Sara walked behind her as they went down a hallway, passing a couple of bookshelves to a room with five computers on two separate tables.

"Choose anyone you want. We don't get many people in here wanting to use the computers. So, don't worry about being interrupted," Laura said.

Sara nodded and took a seat at the first computer at the end of the table.

"Take as long as you need; we're open until 6:00 p.m."

"Thank you," Sara said, before focusing all her attention on the computer in front of her.

She wanted to find out if there was a missing person, preferably a girl who wore a pink coat. Not that it was relevant, but it would help. She typed in Craven Falls, and several articles appeared. The most recent was about several deaths that occurred here in September: a local girl killed under the bleachers at the high school, a boy named Kyle who drowned, and something about his parents being found dead inside the shed in their backyard.

She wondered what the woman's reason was for killing Kyle and the girl. Rage? Jealousy? Sara read on, and she was right. Lianne Fitzgerald killed her stepdaughter, Scarlet, out of jealousy. She had also killed Kyle, who was Scarlet's boyfriend and with whom Lianne had slept with behind Scarlet's back because he was going to reveal their affair. As for Kyle's parents, they were found two months later inside the shed behind their house. The article said nothing about who had killed them.

Sara shuddered at what she'd read on the screen. There was a heaviness in her gut. Her stomach clenched as she absorbed the words, picturing the scene in her mind. She had driven here alone, to this town. She felt nauseous but swallowed several times until she felt a little better. She hadn't done anything wrong, and that wasn't why she felt this way. It was the reality that death seemed to loom over the small town.

Several minutes later, she moved the cursor to the top of the page and typed "*Missing girl in Craven Falls.*"

Nothing.

There wasn't even an article about a girl missing in the local or surrounding area.

Sara leaned back in the chair, staring at the computer screen. She couldn't think of what to type next or what she should search. But she knew one thing: Edith was right about why anyone would want to stay here after all that had happened in the last few months. All the murders would have definitely sent people in her hometown running away for sure.

She decided she'd read through the articles again to see if anything stood out—anything that would help her believe she wasn't losing her mind. That she had, in fact, seen a girl in a pink coat lying half-dead in the road.

Chapter 11

An hour later, Sara was no closer to finding the girl than she had been when she saw her on the road two nights ago. Maybe she had imagined the whole thing. Tired from all the driving and with the rain coming down, it hadn't helped the situation. She had to accept the facts at hand. There was no article about a missing girl. No one else had mentioned her, not that Sara had talked to anyone except Mick and Edith. Though Sara hadn't asked them about a missing girl, either. How would she even approach telling both Edith and Mick what she had seen? Would they think that she was making it up just as she herself believed she had? But everything she had just read on the computer about the recent events here, maybe they would believe her. Perhaps someone else was about to die in this town? If—if they weren't already dead.

Her mind flicked to Laura, who was sitting at the front desk. She could ask her if she had heard or seen anything out of the ordinary, but Sara felt strange asking this girl questions especially since she'd just met her an hour ago. And wasn't her name mentioned in the newspaper clipping she had just read online? She had been a suspect in the girl's death. The one they found under the bleachers. Well, until the police realized that she hadn't done it and found the real killers.

Then it hit her like a burning bag of dog excrement hitting the ground. No one had reported the girl missing yet.

Maybe when Sara had seen her on the road, it had just happened? But two days had gone by. There should have been something reported, wouldn't there? Unless her family didn't know she was missing? But that seemed unlikely to Sara. This was a small town, and she was sure someone would know if their child or teenager was missing. Was she in trouble? Unless they didn't want anyone to know.

Her mind recalled the thoughts she had earlier about her relationship with her mother, the same mother who had left her when she was little. Yet, her mother had recently moved back in with Sara and her grandmother. Sara couldn't take care of her grandmother now that dementia had set in. She was sure her mother probably wouldn't care that she had left. A pang gripped her heart as the words entered her mind. Did her mother miss her? Did she know she had gone? She wanted to believe that she did, but she knew better than to call her. She couldn't reach out because she was sure her mother would tell Brad, and she couldn't give up her hiding spot. Then this would all have been for nothing.

Sara searched for a missing girl from Bristol, but no search results appeared. Well, that answered her question. No one had reported her missing either. Her mother didn't care about her. She was probably glad that Sara had left.

She sat up straight, fighting back sadness and tears, wanting to escape. She didn't understand why she would want to cry over this woman who was her mother. Her mother, who didn't care about her, because if she did, then she would have never left all those years ago. So why should she cry? No one missed her. Well, she doubted that was true. She was sure that Brad missed her and was out there searching for her this very minute.

She deleted the search history and powered down the monitor. Standing up, she exited the room and walked back toward the main lobby where she had entered. Hearing voices, she paused behind a bookshelf labeled Fantasy and Sci-fi.

She looked through the slots above the books and saw Laura talking to another girl. It wasn't Mick; she was certain of that. This girl had blonde hair and a small, round nose. Her eyes sparkled in the luminous light that beamed down from the ceiling. She was pretty.

Sara couldn't hear every word they were saying, but what she did hear was her name. She should have known that her presence here would spread around town. No one shows up and stays hidden. Maybe she should drive back to Edith's, grab her things, and leave, but the sad part was, she didn't want to go. Yet, she couldn't stay. Why couldn't she stay? No one really knew who she was here, but they would find out. They would ask questions, and knowing Sara, she would accidentally let things slip. Things she didn't want them to know, and then they would report her to the police. After that, her mother, if she cared, would come and get her, or would she send Brad? God, she couldn't have Brad find her.

The overwhelming stress was taking a toll on her. She needed to bottle it all inside before she exploded—something she had to do behind closed doors, not in public. She straightened, held her head high, and slipped out from behind the bookshelf. She had no other way out of here except to walk past the front desk where the two girls stood. But before she could slip past unnoticed, Laura spoke.

"Hey, Sara. I want to introduce you to my friend Rachel. Rachel, this is the girl Mick's been nonstop talking about since yesterday."

Sara stopped and turned to face Rachel and Laura. "Hi," Sara said. "It's nice to meet you."

Rachel smiled and stepped closer to Sara. The proximity made Sara feel uneasy. She wasn't one to feel claustrophobic, but she did at that moment.

"It's so nice to meet you, too. Will you be staying here in Craven Falls? I heard you're a senior. We're seniors too," Rachel said, moving her pointer finger from Laura, then back to herself. "Last year of high school, can you believe it?"

Sara shook her head. "No, not really, but looking forward to it being over."

"Yes, don't you agree, Laura? Laura here is moving to North Carolina after high school. I don't want her to go, but I guess it is what it is," Rachel said.

Sara could hear the sadness in Rachel's voice. Was she about to cry over her best friend leaving? Sara hoped not. She didn't handle it well when people started crying; then she would inevitably start crying too. That's why she avoided sad movies in theaters—she was a loud crier. She always waited until they were released on DVD. Besides, she couldn't cry here in front of these two girls; she didn't know them. What would they think of her then?

"North Carolina's a nice place," Sara said, shoving the thoughts to the back of her mind and wanting nothing more than to end the conversation and leave.

"School starts next Monday. You should come with us. We'll introduce you to the rest of the senior class," Rachel said.

"Let me think about it. I'm not sure how long I'm

staying," Sara replied. Laura and Rachel looked at each other, which made Sara feel even more uncomfortable. Had she made a mistake coming to the library? Well, she hadn't known that Laura worked here. Heck, she didn't realize Laura until she got here, so why was she beating herself up? "Well, I should go, Edith is waiting for me to return. I need to help her with some things in the house," Sara said, as she stepped away and toward the main door.

"No problem, maybe we'll stop by sometime and visit with you," Rachel said.

"That would be nice," Sara replied as she slipped through the double doors and back outside into the cold, blistering temperatures.

She skittered down the library steps, pulling her coat tighter around her as she shivered. She hurried across the parking lot to her car and jumped inside, turning the key in the ignition. She had been in the library for at least an hour, and the engine was now cold, as was the interior of the car. The cold leather seats were brutal in the winter. She wondered why her grandmother hadn't wrapped the seats in cotton fabric.

It took nearly five minutes before she felt any warmth blowing from the vent, and then she shifted into reverse and backed out of her spot. When she turned to face out of the car's front windshield, she froze.

Chapter 12

She was sure that it was the girl she had seen lying in the road, but that couldn't be. Could it? Sara threw the car into park and opened the driver's side door. She stood beside the car, looking at this girl. The only thing missing was the pink coat, because this girl was wearing a black coat. Her hood was up over her head, just as it had been that night when she had found her lying in the road. Her hair looked brown, maybe a dark red, but she couldn't be sure from this distance. Sara glanced down at the girl's leg, but she saw nothing wrong. There was no blood, nor were her jeans torn. She didn't see any obvious signs of a broken leg. Sara opened her mouth to say something when she heard someone call out to her.

"Sara, are you alright?"

Sara turned, looked behind her, and toward the voice. It was Rachel. She stood on the steps at the bottom of the library entrance. Sara redirected her gaze back to the girl in the black coat, but she had vanished. Sara spun around in circles, but she didn't see her anywhere. Only two other cars were parked in the huge parking lot, located on the other side of Sara's car, making it unlikely that she would hide beside the vehicles.

Sara looked into the woods across the parking lot but didn't see anyone running or even walking toward or within them.

"Sara," Rachel said as she approached and stood next to

her. "Is everything okay?"

Sara looked at Rachel and then over her shoulder again. "I… I thought I saw someone. Didn't you see her?"

"See who?"

A girl in a black coat stood right in front of my car.

Rachel shook her head. "No. There was no one out here when I came outside. I saw you get out of your car, and you were standing there. I don't know, like you were in a trance." She touched a hand to Sara's arm.

Although the touch was innocent, she jumped back and rammed her spine into the metal frame of the car, wincing. "You didn't see anyone?" Sara questioned, her voice rising as pain shot down her back.

Rachel dropped her hand from Sara's arm and stepped back as if Sara had smacked her across the face. "No. I didn't see anyone, Sara," Rachel's voice trembled as if she were fighting back tears. "Do… do you want to go back inside? Should I call someone to come and get you?"

"No!" Sara snapped, then she realized what she had done.

"I'm sorry," Rachel said. "I didn't mean to upset you."

Sara closed her eyes, letting herself calm down. "No, I'm sorry. Really, I am. I didn't mean to yell at you. Do you swear that you didn't see that girl?"

Rachel replied, "I swear, I didn't see anyone," while scanning the scenery.

Sara knew she was losing it. She was seeing things that weren't there, which was probably what had happened two nights ago when she arrived. There was nobody in the road; she had made the whole thing up. Her mind was exhausted, and she was hallucinating. She was scared that Brad would find her and kill her. Now, she was doing the same thing. There had never been anyone in front of her car minutes ago.

"I need to go," Sara said as she slipped back inside the car and slammed the door shut. She shifted into drive and headed toward Edith's house, leaving Rachel standing behind her in the freezing cold.

She pulled into the driveway and drove past the length of Edith's house until she spotted the garage. From here, no one would notice the car from the road, which was exactly what Sara wanted. She parked the car and turned off the ignition, but she didn't get out. Instead, she just sat there and stared out the windshield. Her eyes shifted to the chain hanging from the rearview mirror. Instinctively, her hand went to it, touching the cold silver engraving.

"Had I seen that girl in the road, or was my mind playing tricks on me?" she whispered into the car. The half-heart necklace stared back at her.

Her mind drifted back to that night. She had touched the girl's neck. She had felt a pulse—she was sure of it. *Was any of it real?* She wondered. It had to be real. There was no way her mind had conjured the entire scene, no matter how tired and scared she had felt that night.

A loud pounding sound startled her, causing her to jump in her seat, her heart galloping like a horse racing to the finish line. She turned to look out the driver's side window. Mick stood outside, motioning for her to roll down the window. Sara grabbed her purse and opened the door.

"What are you doing out here?" Mick asked.

Sara climbed out of the car and closed the door. "I was just thinking."

"Well, can't you do your thinking inside where it's

warm?" Mick joked. "It's freaking freezing out here. God, I swear it's like -15 degrees. It hurts my teeth if I open my mouth."

Sara felt her head nodding up and down, agreeing with Mick even though she hadn't been listening to her. She felt as if she were somewhere else, not standing outside in the wintry air that made her lick her lips and turned her nose redder than Rudolph's.

Mick linked her arm around Sara's and tugged her toward the house. "Come on, it's colder than cow balls out here."

Sara snapped out of her thoughts and laughed at this. She laughed so hard that she had to stop walking because her stomach hurt, and she bent over in the driveway.

"What is so funny?" Mick asked.

Sara regained her composure. "Well," she cleared her throat. "How do you know that cow balls are cold?"

A second later, Mick laughed. "I hadn't really thought about that before. I just come up with certain things and say them. Even if they make little sense."

They giggled together as they walked up the stairs and entered through the back door of the house.

Edith was in the kitchen preparing a chicken pot pie when they entered the room, still laughing at what Mick had said.

"What's so funny, girls?" Edith asked.

The two girls exchanged glances, as if silently agreeing not to tell Edith the joke.

"We're just having fun, Edith," Sara said. There was no way she could say those words to her. Edith was a kind old woman and was sure she wouldn't find any humor in the joke.

I'm glad to see you've made a friend here in Craven Falls.

Sara smiled at this. She thought the same thing.

"Will you be staying for dinner, Mick?" Edith asked.

"Sure, I'll just text Mabel and let her know. Don't need her thinking something bad happened to me."

Sara looked over at Mick. Who was Mabel? Should she ask? And why would Mick even think that something bad would happen to her? Then she thought back to earlier when she had read what had transpired in this town over the last couple of months. She decided she would ask Mick later. She was just glad that she had made a friend.

After Mick finished texting, they went upstairs to the room where Sara was staying.

"Can you tell me about this town?" Sara asked. She wanted to hear it from Mick because she knew that newspapers sometimes exaggerated the truth.

"What do you mean?" Mick asked.

"Well, I went to the library today, and I read online that there were some people killed here."

Mick nodded and began telling Sara everything that she knew. "I didn't become friends with Laura and Rachel until after what had happened to… I can't speak her name. It was the most horrifying thing that has ever happened in this town, and I've lived here my whole life."

Sara knew it was time to ask Mick if he had heard of anyone living here who wore a pink coat. After the words formed in her head, they sounded stupid. Mick would think she was a nutcase and tell all his friends about her. And if she stayed, she would need friends. Well, she didn't need them, but she would feel more comfortable having some friends. So, she would wait until she knew more, if there was anything more to know, especially after what had happened at the library with Rachel not seeing the girl. Sara was sure her mind hadn't really seen her either.

Chapter 13

As the next few days passed, Sara and Mick spent more time together at Edith's house. Sara contributed by cleaning the house and cooking the meals so that Edith could relax. This place felt like home. She had a home with her grandmother, but this was different somehow. She loved living with Edith, and she got the impression that Edith enjoyed her company, too.

When Monday arrived, Sara and Mick drove to school together. Mick walked Sara to the office.

"I'll see you at lunchtime, unless they put you in one of my classes," Mick said as she said goodbye to Sara, leaving her alone in the office.

Sara sat in the chair, waiting for the woman behind the counter to ask her what she needed. Five minutes had passed before they acknowledged her.

"What can I help you with this morning?" a petite woman with glasses asked from behind the counter.

Sara stood up and walked to the desk. "Hi, I'm new here."

"Do you have your transcripts?"

"No." Sara felt her insides turn.

"Well," the woman said. "Give me the last school you attended, and we'll call and have them fax over your transcripts. Is your mother here with you?"

Sara shook her head.

"How old are you?"

Sara swallowed, knowing she couldn't lie. "Seventeen."

"Well, call your mother or your guardian and have them come in and sign some papers while I call for your transcripts."

Sara felt sick—sicker than she had ever felt before. She knew that if this woman called her old school, wouldn't her old school then call her grandmother and ask her questions? Then her mom and grandmother would know where she was, and she couldn't let that happen. If that happened, Brad would find out, and he would come here to drag her back to Bristol, or… or he would kill her and bury her in the woods here in Craven Falls, where no one would ever find her. She didn't know what she would do. She couldn't let them call. Her head ached. It was too much.

"Miss? Hello, are you alright?" the petite woman asked.

Sara snapped out of her thoughts. "Yes, I'm fine." But she wasn't fine. The temperature in the room was rising. Sweat beaded on her forehead and along her hairline. Her lips tingled, and acid surged in the back of her throat. Was she about to puke?

"Okay, well, give me your information, and I'll contact your old school."

"I don't feel so good," Sara said as she turned, bolted out the main door, and into the blistering cold air. She quickened her pace to the side of the building and retched into the bushes. She held onto the wall with one hand as her knees felt weak and wobbly.

"Can I help you?" a voice said from behind her. "Can I get someone?"

Sara wiped her lips and chin before turning to the person behind her. It was Laura from the library.

"Oh, my God, you're white as snow. Here, let me help you. Do you want me to take you home?"

"I can drive," Sara said, but she knew there was no way in hell she could get behind the wheel. Even though Edith's house was only a couple of minutes down the road, she couldn't be sure she would get there safely.

"No way are you driving!" Laura stammered. "I'll take you."

Laura wrapped her arm around Sara and guided her to the parking lot, finally helping her into Laura's car. Within a few minutes, Sara was back at Edith's, resting in her bed upstairs with a bucket beside her.

She hadn't felt this sick since she drank a whole bottle of cinnamon Jägermeister at a party last summer. It was a dare she had taken, and she thought for sure that she would die the next day. She was sick for two days and swore she would never drink like that again. That was also when Brad noticed her for the first time. He called her the next day, but she was still out of commission. By that Wednesday, she returned his call and went out on a date with him. He picked her up around five on Saturday evening and took her to dinner at an expensive Japanese restaurant in Niles. She wasn't a fan of the food but ate what she could as she didn't want to disappoint him. They then went to see a movie, and he took her home afterward. He kissed her goodnight. The next day he called her, and they went out again. They became a couple within a week, and several months later, she saw the real him, but she was too afraid to leave him. She was scared that he would hurt her worse than he already had; besides, she loved him.

Covering the bruises was easy, but the trauma took a toll

on her. Her thinking became distorted, and her grades fell. She was failing all but one class. She had been an outstanding student until she started dating Brad. Her teachers asked her to stay after class, inquiring if things were okay at home but not once asking if everything was good with Brad. Would she have confided in any of the teachers if they had asked? Probably not, but the choice would have been hers to make.

She had hidden in the stalls of the girls' locker room so no one would see the bruises under her clothes. She wore sweatpants instead of shorts in P.E., and long sleeves seemed to be her go-to for shirts, even if the weather was too warm for them, which it had been. When her friends asked her why she was wearing long sleeves, she just told them that she was cold, which she was because Brad had also told her that she was fat, and she had starved herself. Though she hadn't weighed over one hundred and eleven pounds, which with her height was already too skinny.

As Sara lay in bed, under the warmth of the covers, staring up at the ceiling, she knew she couldn't take the chance of Brad finding her. This meant she wouldn't be attending school in Craven Falls.

Chapter 14

The next morning when Sara woke, she nearly jumped out of her skin when she saw Mick sitting at the foot of the bed, staring at her.

"Oh good, you're up," Mick said, as if she had just entered the room, which she hadn't, since she had been sitting on the bed for the last ten minutes.

"You scared the shit out of me!" Sara shouted as she pushed herself up to a sitting position. "What are you doing here?" Her heart felt as if it were about to claw its way out from under her skin and burst.

"I came to see how you were feeling. I heard what happened to you yesterday, and Laura said she brought you home. Are you feeling better?"

"I was until you scared the crap out of me," Sara said, trying to calm her voice.

"Sorry, I didn't mean to. Edith said I could come upstairs, and you were sleeping. I didn't want to bother you. I figured I would wait until you woke up," Mick replied, a smile unfolding on her lips.

Sara leaned back against the headboard. "No, I'm sorry. I shouldn't have yelled at you. You have been nothing but kind since I arrived here." Yet, yelling seemed to be all she had done when Rachel and Mick were only trying to help her.

"Yeah, but I shouldn't have been sitting up here waiting for you to wake up," Mick replied as she stood. "I guess I didn't realize that I would startle you when you woke, seeing someone sitting at the edge of the bed. Sorry. I'll let you get dressed for school. Are you going to school? I should have asked that first," Mick laughed.

"What time is it?"

"Almost six thirty in the morning, so you have some time to shower and get dressed. I'll be downstairs talking with Edith."

"Oh, okay," Sara said. She wasn't sure how to explain to Mick that she wasn't going to school because if she gave the office her information, she would give herself away. She recalled what Laura had said about confiding in Mick with her secrets. She couldn't let anyone find out the truth about her and why she was here. She wasn't certain what excuse she would give Mick, but she had to come up with one quickly.

✢ ✢ ✢

Less than twenty minutes later, Sara came down the stairs with a white cotton robe wrapped around her. She walked into the kitchen, where she found both Edith and Mick sitting at the table, chatting.

"Why aren't you dressed?" Mick asked.

"I'm still not feeling well," Sara lied. "Once I started moving around, I felt sick again, so I think it's best if I stay home for another day. Maybe I have the flu or something?" Sara said.

"Oh, no," Edith replied. "You poor, dear. I can make you some chicken soup for lunch later."

"Thank you, that'd be nice. But please don't go to too much trouble. I'll be fine."

"Nonsense, dear. You have taken care of me over the last

couple of days. Now it's my turn," Edith smiled.

Sara nodded.

"Well, I should start heading to school then," Mick said. "I hope that you feel better. I can stop by after school before I go to work."

"Oh, you don't need to do that. I don't want you catching whatever I have," Sara replied. She wanted Mick to stop by, but she had to play this flu illness off as if it were real. She couldn't return to that school. She couldn't let them find her here.

"Oh, okay. Well, either way, I'll see you around," Mick said.

Sara could hear the disappointment in Mick's voice. She needed to say something to ensure that Mick knew they were friends, but what could she say to resolve this? She didn't know, but her opportunity was running out as Mick opened the front door and stood on the porch.

"Just stop by before you go to work tonight. I may feel better, and besides, I'd like to see you again," Sara said, as the cold wind bit at her face, making her gasp and hide behind the door.

A smile spread across Mick's face, and Sara knew that she had won her over. Sara watched as Mick climbed down the wooden porch stairs. They waved at one another before Mick turned away, made her way down the sidewalk, and walked in the direction of the school.

Sara found it odd that Mick didn't have a car, especially in this kind of weather. In fact, it hadn't crossed Sara's mind until now that she didn't even know where Mick lived. Mick had always come to Edith's house. She would have to remember to ask Mick later, but it really wasn't any of her business, was it? Well, technically not, but she still wanted to know where the girl lived. What kind of house did she live in?

Sara closed the door, locked it, and walked back toward the kitchen where Edith was still sitting. She grabbed a ceramic cup from the cabinet, poured herself a cup of coffee, and sat down across from Edith.

"So, are you going to tell me what's going on with you, and why you can't tell the school your address? Where did you come from?" Edith asked, looking down at the newspaper open on the table in front of her. "I know you're not sick with the flu."

Sara's mouth dropped open, but she closed it before Edith lifted her head to look at her.

"I know something is going on with you. You can trust me; I won't tell anyone. It won't leave this room," Edith said, as she looked at Sara with her kind and caring eyes.

Could Sara trust this woman? She didn't have to think long to know that she could. This woman had allowed her into her home and she had been staying here for a few days. Yes, she could trust her. Edith was trustworthy, and Sara could tell this all by talking to her.

Her hands were shaking before a word even slipped from her tongue. "I ran away from home," Sara whispered. She kept her hands in her lap beneath the table, away from Edith's observing eyes. Should she let this woman know she was afraid? Just how scared was she for her life?

No, she wasn't sure she should share that part. Maybe she would only tell her what she needed to know. Besides, she didn't want Edith's life to be in danger. There was no telling what Brad would do to her if he knew that she had confided in this woman. Sara wouldn't be able to live with Edith's blood on her hands, but that was only if she survived herself. There would be nothing to stop Brad from killing her, too.

Chapter 15

Sara excluded Brad from her conversation and spoke only of her mother. She fabricated a story about her mother being a drunk who was never present to care for her.

"Oh, I'm so sorry to hear that, Sara. Well, you can stay here as long as you want to. Now, let's figure out how we can get you enrolled in school."

"Really?" Sara cheered.

"Yes, of course. Did you think you'd stay here and not finish school?"

"Well, I just don't know how I will get those transcript papers I need. The school won't let me in until they have them."

"You let me worry about that. I have a friend here in town who can help with that," Edith said, smiling.

Sara jumped up from her chair and wrapped her arms around Edith. "Thank you, thank you, thank you," Sara said a little too loudly in Edith's ear.

"Calm down, my dear," Edith laughed, pulling away. "I'll make a call and have you in school first thing tomorrow."

Sara towered above Edith with a smile on her face. She wasn't sure why she felt so happy about going to school tomorrow. Most kids would be thrilled to stay home, but sitting here in this house day after day made Sara feel claustrophobic. She needed to get out of the house and be around other people. Not that she didn't enjoy Edith's company.

✢ ✢ ✢

Later that morning, Sara showered and got dressed. A walk was what she needed to clear her mind and forget about what had brought her to this town: Edith's house. She felt it was a new beginning, a do-over. She knew she could be herself here because no one knew her or what she was running from.

She was glad that her ankle no longer hurt as she walked past the buildings in town and down the next street. After her walk, she decided to stop at the school to retrieve the car she had left there yesterday.

The houses receded further as she walked out of town. Birds chirped all around her, singing their songs and conversing with one another. It felt peaceful out here, a sensation she hadn't experienced since her arrival. She knew she couldn't return to Bristol if Brad was still alive. He wouldn't let her be without him, especially knowing what she knew, what she saw.

She would stay here in Craven Falls. A place she could not only make a home, but call home. Then again, there wasn't much here in the lines of work. Either way, she could live here and work outside of town, right? It was definitely something she could consider later. She wanted to enjoy her walk in the quietness that surrounded her.

Up ahead, she spotted something unexpected—something most people wouldn't notice while walking in the country. Bright yellow caution tape lay across the end of a driveway. Sara walked to the mailbox, where the name written on it had been spray-painted over. She opened the small metal door and reached inside, pulling out a handful of envelopes. Each envelope had **Tanner** written on it.

Tanner? Where had she seen that name before? Her mind shuffled through the days she had spent in Craven Falls, recalling her visit to the library and the conversation she had with Mick. Someone had murdered the Tanner family.

Sara's mind wanted to know more about what had happened, but what else was there to discover? Someone had killed Kyle, and they found his parents in the shed behind their house—end of story. Yet, there was something drawing her to this house. Something wanted her here, but what?

Her mind flicked back to the night she had arrived, when she had supposedly seen a body in the road: a girl wearing a pink winter coat. Then, at the library, as she was leaving, she thought she saw a girl standing in front of her car, but Rachel said there was no one there. Rachel wouldn't have lied to her, would she? No, she was sure Rachel had been telling the truth because why would she lie about something like that? This uncertainty haunted her more and more with each passing day. Sara needed to find out the truth. She needed to know about this girl in the pink coat.

Then it hit her. Should she look for someone who was wearing the other half of the heart necklace she had found? Yes, she could do that, but what were the chances of finding that person? And what if there were more than one person in this town who wore the same necklace? Did the girl wearing the other half live here? What if she had been visiting relatives and lived in another town? And let's say that she came across a girl wearing the other half; then what? She couldn't come right out and ask this girl where she got the necklace or what the name of this best friend was. Could she?

Well, she would first have to find the best friend with the other half of the heart before deciding what to do. But at that very moment, she had nothing to go on. She was merely speculating. Her mind wanted to come up with an answer to her minor situation, but to her, it wasn't minor. Not if this girl in the pink coat needed her help.

Then another question formed in her mind. If this girl needed or wanted Sara's help, why had she run from her? This she didn't know, but she would find the answers. She would look for this girl in the pink coat, and she would help her.

Sara shoved the envelopes back inside the mailbox and walked over to the caution tape that hung loosely across the driveway. It wasn't just a spur-of-the-moment walk down the wooded road that had brought her here. No, there was something out here that wanted her to come, and only her, as if it were calling her name.

Gravel crunched under her boots as she walked up the S-shaped driveway. A house appeared before her. It was a two-story home with a wrap-around porch on one side. She recognized not only from the caution tape laced across the driveway, but also from the emptiness of how the house appeared from where she stood. To her, the house looked sad, something she was sure a home couldn't feel. A house like this needed a family to live in it, to give it love and life.

She continued forward, as if something or someone were pulling her toward the house. She climbed the wooden stairs, the boards whining and creaking under her weight. She stopped at the front door but didn't try it to see if it was unlocked. Instead, she made her way around the house.

In front of her, she spotted a pool with soggy brown and

orange leaves floating across the water, dropped from the trees surrounding the house. Then, her eyes caught a glimpse of the shed in the distance. The article she had read at the library, along with Mick's story, entered her mind. She fixed the details of the scene in her head until she could visualize every aspect of the Tanner family and how they had died. Her stomach flipped as nausea swept through her body. She had to erase the memory of what had happened to them, or she would be sick again—not that she had anything in her stomach, as she hadn't eaten breakfast this morning, just coffee.

She inhaled deeply, then swallowed, wishing she had water to help wash down the bile that was inching its way up her esophagus to her mouth, back down where it belonged.

Several minutes later, after closing her eyes and taking a few deep breaths, she felt better. She stepped forward and walked around the pool, taking the stairs down to the ground and into the backyard. She passed the area where the logs were blackened and burnt from a long-ago bonfire.

She stopped visualizing the scene. She was sure she could hear the voices of the teenagers talking and laughing all around her as they drank from red solo cups. The fire crackled as red-hot ashes drifted into the air before fizzling out and disappearing into thin air. Music played in the distance, loud enough to make her heart feel like it would explode from under her rib cage. It reminded her of the parties she had once gone to with her girlfriends.

She closed her eyes, and when she opened them, the sounds she thought she heard and felt had disappeared. There was no one out here, no party, no music, and definitely no fire burning. No teenagers were dancing or laughing. She was alone, out here in the woods.

She navigated around the charred wood and entered the woods. It felt as if a force was pulling her along, as if she had no control over her actions, like a robot being directed by someone else.

Branches snapped beneath her feet as she climbed the small incline. She held onto the sapling trees to prevent slipping—or worse, falling back down the hill. Not that she would fall far, but she couldn't allow herself to get hurt out here. No one knew she was here. She had just gone out for a walk and discovered this place. It would worry Edith sick if she didn't return home. Then Edith would call the police and have them search for her. She should just turn around and go back before something happened. She wanted to forget about this place, but she couldn't. She needed to continue to the top, and then she would go home. She would return to Edith's.

Once she was on the other side, she saw a pile of dirt. This frazzled her because she wondered why there would be a mound of dirt. *Unless it was a grave?* She questioned.

She stepped closer. The dirt lay piled beside an open hole in the ground. She cautiously approached the hole, then halted.

Chapter 16

Sara couldn't scream. The sound lodged in her throat, sealed shut like tuna in a can. She had no idea that when she left the house this morning and went for a walk, she would stumble across this house. That she would come out into these woods and find what she had discovered in the hole in front of her. Had she known all of this, she would have stayed in bed under the warmth of the blankets or curled up on the sofa by the fireplace, chatting with Edith. But she hadn't known.

She swallowed, but there was no keeping the sour, acidic bile down this time. She turned and hurried over to a tree. With one hand gripping the tree bark, she placed her other hand around her stomach as she vomited violently. The coffee she drank this morning burned as it sprayed out of her nose and mouth. The wind blew, causing the smell to linger in her nose. She heaved again until there was nothing left inside her. She let out a few more dry heaves and then leaned her body against the tree, feeling exhausted, before wiping her mouth with the back of her gloved hand.

She wasn't sure if she could walk back over to the hole and look down at the body she had seen. The body that looked like a girl who had been there for how long, she wasn't sure. She didn't know how long it took a body to decompose, and she didn't really care to find out. But if she had to guess how long this girl had been dead, had been in this hole in the ground between warm and freezing temperatures, she would say at least a week.

Once the thought had entered her mind, she knew it had been around the time she arrived here. Had it been the same night she drove into town? The same night she had apparently seen the body in the road? Were they linked? She didn't know, but a part of her believed something connected them. One thing was for certain: she knew it wasn't the girl she had seen on the road. The girl in the grave wasn't wearing a pink coat or a black one. Her coat was red. Maybe she had thought the coat was pink, but in fact, it was red? It was probable. They were similar in color. It had been dark and stormy out. Anyone could have made that mistake.

The more she replayed the scene of that night in her head, the more she believed that she had seen a red coat instead of a pink one. She thought the girl had gotten up and run into the woods, fell into the hole on her back, and died—instantly. She knew this because she saw the dry blood on the shirt she was wearing and in the hole.

But that didn't explain why there wasn't a broken leg, she thought. As much as she wanted to stand here and figure out if she were the same girl from a week ago, she couldn't just do nothing. She needed to call for help. Her hand automatically slipped inside her coat pocket for her cell phone, but it wasn't there. It was still in the glove compartment in her car, which was back at school and probably dead, just like this girl in front of her.

She wanted to scream, to let out all her anger. But what good would that do? It wouldn't solve the problem of not having her phone with her because she was living in fear of Brad finding her. She hadn't dared to turn the cell phone back on and disable the Find My Phone feature, the one thing he could use to locate her and know where she was at all times. Right there should have alarmed her that he was controlling, but it hadn't. Or maybe she just didn't want to see the real him because she loved him.

But she couldn't worry about that now. She had to go back and get help. She couldn't leave this girl here as if she hadn't found her. Though Sara was afraid to leave, a part of her feared that when she returned with help, the body would disappear as if it had never existed, like the body in the road, which had vanished. However, the girl was here and wouldn't be going anywhere this time. Sara was sure of this.

She decided to go for help when she heard a twig snap behind her. Her face became hot and flushed. The cold 20 degrees didn't cool her down or stop the sweat from forming; it rolled beneath her shirt and between the breasts of her padded bra.

She stood up straight, rooted to the spot where she was, and stared ahead. Her ears perked up, and her head turned slightly, as if she were a deer frozen in the headlights of an oncoming car.

She took a deep breath, held it, and listened.

Behind her.

She heard another branch snap.

She swallowed, nearly choking on the breath caught in her lungs.

She twisted around without moving her feet, afraid to make a sound. As she turned her neck, positioning her head in the direction of the noise, she saw who it was and let out the air that she had held inside. The tension left her body as if it were all a bad dream.

"Mick, what the hell are you doing out here?" Sara asked

as she allowed herself to relax, now that she knew who was behind her. "You scared the living shit out of me."

"I could ask you the same question?" Mick replied as she came closer. A look of disgust crossed her face as she pinched her nose between her forefinger and thumb. She turned to the left, then back at Sara. "Oh, my God, are you okay?"

Sara nodded. "I'm fine now, but do you have a phone on you?"

"Yes, why?"

"We need to call for help," Sara said.

Mick looked at Sara for a long minute, her eyes moving up and down her body before she answered. "Why? You don't look hurt."

"It's not me that needs help," Sara replied, then turned her head toward the hole.

Mick approached Sara and looked down at the ground in front of them.

Sara looked over and saw Mick's eyes widen, wondering if she would feel sick too. However, she didn't run away or scream. Instead, she just stood there, silent and shell-shocked by what lay in front of her. Neither of them said a word as Mick pulled her cell phone out of the pocket of her fluffy, white winter coat, which reminded Sara of an Eskimo, and dialed for help.

Chapter 17

The girls stood to the side while two police officers took pictures before lifting the body out of the hole and placing it on the ground outside the grave. Sara heard Mick gasp and turned to look at her.

"What is it, Mick?" Sara asked.

"I… I know that girl," Mick replied. "Her name is Megan. She goes to my school. I mean, she went to my school, but I thought she moved away last week."

"Are you sure?" Sara asked.

"Yeah, I'm sure it's her. She doesn't have any siblings, at least none that I know of. Crystal will be so devastated."

"Who's Crystal?"

Megan's aunt is a police officer here in town. Her sister Delaney, Megan's mom, supposedly moved the week before Thanksgiving—right when you showed up here," Mick said.

They both turned when they heard a noise from the other side of the hill.

"Oh, shit," Mick muttered.

Sara was about to ask, but then figured it out on her own when she noticed a woman in a police uniform. "Is that the woman you were talking about?" Sara asked.

Mick nodded.

Both Sara and Mick stood still, watching as Officer Crystal Rosmus walked past them toward the body that the other officers had lifted out of the grave.

Sara wasn't sure, but she could have sworn she heard the

name *"Robyn"* come out of the officer's mouth.

Mick had said it was Megan, not Robyn? She knew she hadn't misheard the words Mick had spoken. Or maybe Mick was wrong, and Megan had a sister or a relative who looked exactly like her? Sara didn't know this, as she had just arrived in town, but she was sure they were about to find out soon enough. Something had happened here, and Sara wasn't going to stop until she found out the truth.

Sara watched as Officer Rosmus turned to look at them after one of the other officers pointed in their direction. Officer Rosmus then walked over to where they were standing.

"Which one of you found the body?"

"I did," Sara replied, raising her hand as if she were in middle school.

"Is it Megan?" Mick asked.

Officer Rosmus didn't answer the question; instead, she asked a different one. "I haven't seen you in Craven Falls before. What's your name? And why were you out here in these woods?" Officer Romus wore no smile. Her demeanor gave off signs of a bully.

Sara felt as if she were being interrogated and didn't know how to answer the questions thrown at her. Didn't she have the right not to answer them? She'd watched shows on television where the person being questioned had the right to speak only to their attorney, but she had done nothing wrong. Why would she need an attorney? She couldn't afford one. She couldn't let the police run her name; then she'd have to pack her things and escape to another town. She would have to keep running until no one questioned her identity, which she knew would never stop. She should have given Mick and

Edith a false name. Dammit! Why didn't she provide them with a different name?

"I… I arrived here last week. I'm staying with Edith; she owns the Bed and Breakfast here in town," Sara said.

"I know who Edith is!" Officer Rosmus barked.

Sara stepped back as if punched in the gut. She hadn't implied that the officer didn't know who Edith was; she was only stating the facts. Sara wouldn't have known if more than one Edith were living in town.

"So, what were you doing out at the Tanner house? Out in these woods?" Rosmus asked.

Sara wasn't sure what to tell this officer. Should she tell her the truth? Start from the very beginning when she arrived here on that stormy night last week. No, she didn't want to mention that night. It would only lead to more questions, and Sara didn't want more questions. She didn't want any of this. She just wanted to escape from Brad.

"I don't know. I was going for a walk, and I saw the house. Something drew me out here. I can't explain it," Sara said. Though she wasn't lying; something had drawn her out here.

"And you, Mickey? What were you doing out here?" Officer Rosmus asked. "Your aunt would have your hind if she knew you were at the Tanner house after what had happened here. You of all people should know better."

"I followed her," Mick replied, tilting her head toward Sara.

Officer Rosmus seemed to accept both their answers. "Okay, so you came out into these woods, and you found the body just like it was?"

Sara nodded.

"You didn't touch the body?"

Sara shook her head.

"Is it Megan?" Mick asked again.

"I'm not releasing the girl's name until a thorough investigation has been done," Officer Rosmus said.

"So, it isn't Megan?" Mick questioned.

"Mickey, I'm not telling you anything," Officer Rosmus growled.

"But she looks like Megan. You would know if she's your niece," Mick stated.

"Again, this is none of your business, young lady. Once we take the body to the morgue, we will do an autopsy to find the cause of death. Then we will go from there."

Sara knew the cause of death. The body had fallen into the hole; however, had it fallen in, or had she been placed there? Sara wasn't certain, but she was sure that no one had put the body there. Did it even matter how it got there? No, but it was clear how the girl had died. She had landed on her back, and a two-inch-thick root had pierced through her back and out the front, in the same area as her heart.

So, there wouldn't need to be an autopsy unless—unless they wanted to know if the girl was on drugs or something. Yes, that was possible. She could have been out in these woods, stumbled, and fallen into the hole. The hole that someone had dug, which had just occurred to Sara. This brought on more questions, to which she had no answers. Did it have anything to do with the night she arrived? Was that why the girl in the pink was running? It was possible.

"You two head back into town, and we will handle this. If I have any more questions, I know where to find you," Officer Rosmus said. "Just make sure you don't go anywhere. What was your name again?"

Sara hadn't provided the officer with her name, and she didn't want to. She was apprehensive about the officer checking her name in the database and discovering that she was a runaway, and then what? Well, she knew what would come next, Brad. "Sara."

"Sara, what?" Officer Rosmus asked.

Sara knew she didn't have to give this officer her last name and wasn't going to. She had rights, didn't she?

"Just, Sara."

Sara grabbed Mick's arm and led her back down the hill toward the Tanner house from which she had come. It took them a little over twenty minutes to return to the school and get Sara's car. With the temperatures in the low teens, the girls didn't have the energy to walk any faster. It was as if she had entered a different world, like death had taken over in this town.

She pulled into the driveway at Edith's and parked the car. "Do you want me to drive you home?" Sara asked. "It's way too cold to walk, especially since we just walked from the Tanner house."

Mick shook her head. "No, I'm good. It's not that far."

Sara wanted to say that she would drive her, but got the impression that Mick didn't want her to know where she lived. But why? How horrible could her place be? Sara had seen the houses in town; they all looked better than average. Were there less livable homes? She didn't know because she hadn't explored all the streets in Craven Falls.

"I'll be fine," Mick said before turning and walking away from Edith's house.

Sara wanted to stand there and watch which way Mick

turned, but Mick must have known this because she crossed the street and went into Falls Café. So, Sara headed up the walk and into the bed-and-breakfast.

Chapter 18

Sara rose early the following morning and got dressed for her first day of school at CFH. Edith had given Sara, as promised, a file with signed transcripts inside, without further questions. She knew she owed Edith so much for doing this and for whoever had helped obtain the documents for her. She wasn't sure if she should ask Edith who had done this, but Sara decided that she had secrets too, and this unknown person deserved to keep their identity private.

Mick arrived a few minutes before Sara was set to leave, and they rode together.

"You know I could have picked you up," Sara suggested to Mick as she drove out of the driveway and turned right.

"It's no problem. I don't mind walking to Edith's house."

"Yeah, but doesn't it defeat the purpose of me giving you a ride to school if you have to walk to get the ride?" Sara questioned. From the corner of her eye, she saw Mick shrug her shoulders and look out the passenger window. She wanted to know more about her, but Mick was as sealed up as packaged cheese. "I just want you to know that you can talk to me about anything. I don't judge people."

Mick seemed to nod at this.

"Well, okay then, thanks for the talk," Sara laughed as she turned into the parking lot of the school and parked the car. They had arrived early so Sara could go to the office and get her schedule.

They both opened the car doors simultaneously and walked into the school. Although Sara knew where to find the front office, Mick accompanied her. After they finished, Mick showed Sara where her locker was since classes didn't start for another fifteen minutes.

"It looks like we have two classes together," Mick smiled at this. "You also have classes with Laura and Rachel. They will help you with anything you need. We can all sit together at lunch if you'd like. This will be so much fun." Mick gleamed with joy.

Sara was getting just as excited as Mick about being here and having classes together. A part of her missed her old friends and wondered what they were doing and if they thought of her, as she thought of them. But she couldn't dwell on them right now. She had to leave her friends behind and start over with a new life. It wasn't just her friends at that school; Brad was there too. She wouldn't ever go back. This was her new home, thanks to Edith.

Mick and Sara went their separate ways minutes before the first bell rang. Sara followed Mick's directions, walking down the hall and turning right, then down another hallway. Before she entered the classroom, she heard a girl with short, wavy brown hair and braces mention something about a girl in her class who was missing. Sara stopped dead in her tracks and slinked off to the side, away from the flow of other students making their way down the hall. She pretended to read her schedule while listening to the girl's conversation.

"Did you hear about the girl that they found in the woods yesterday?" asked the girl with brown hair. "The police have been keeping it hush, hush, but everyone here in town is talking. Even Officer Rosmus told me not to talk to people about her, but I think we should be worried. You know, with all the so-called deaths happening here in town lately."

"Yeah, especially since Scarlet," her friend with auburn hair replied, as she looked around with enquiring eyes and then continued. "I can't believe they don't want us to know. I mean, shouldn't they want to keep us safe from whoever is doing this? Even Megan and her mom have left town. So, that means that Officer Rosmus knows what's going on."

Sara jumped when the bell sounded. Although she wanted to listen and find out more, she knew she shouldn't be late for her first class, even though she was standing right outside the classroom door. She was certain that the conversation was about the girl she had found the previous day. Was the dead girl connected to the one she had seen on the road? If so, Sara wanted to find out more about her. Did she own a pink coat? Who was she friends with here at school? She knew by the appearance of the two girls that they were a couple of grades below her. Maybe they were ninth or tenth graders? She didn't know, but she would find out. And she knew just who to ask.

\+ + +

Hours later, Sara walked into the cafeteria looking for Mick, whom she spotted sitting at a table a few rows away. There was no one else sitting with him, which meant it was the perfect time to ask him questions.

"Hi, how were your classes this morning?" Mick asked as Sara walked up to the table.

"They were good." She didn't want to discuss school-related matters. "Hey, did you hear anything more about the girl we found in the woods yesterday?" Sara whispered as she leaned across the table so only Mick could hear.

Mick shook her head. "Nothing since talking to Officer Rosmus yesterday. Why did you hear something?" Mick asked, as she also moved her eyes around the room to see if anyone was listening.

Sara thought for a minute, wondering if she should mention what she had heard from those two girls in the hall earlier this morning, even though they hadn't said anything she didn't already know. They hadn't revealed who the girl was that they had found.

As usual, she felt like she was back to square one, but she would have to keep her ears and eyes open. She would go back to the Tanner house, and this time she would enter the house. She was sure that if there were someone else out there, they wouldn't be living outside in the cold. What better place to hide than the Tanner house, where no one lived? No one would go to look for them.

Chapter 19

After Sara dropped Mick off at work, she drove to the Tanner house. When she arrived, the caution tape was blowing in the wind, no longer slack across the driveway. She didn't hesitate and drove up the winding driveway. The gravel crunched under the tires, creating popping sounds. If she were trying to be quiet, it wasn't working.

The house came into view, and from where she sat, it looked different somehow—less eerie than the day before. Although she had paid little attention to the details of the house like she was right now, yesterday she felt almost comatose. Moving around the outside of the perimeter and into the woods felt like something was pulling her out there. She couldn't explain it and was glad no one had asked her to.

There were no police cars in the driveway or by the garage; however, if there had been, she would have slammed the car into reverse and hightailed it out of the driveway before anyone saw her. But she was the only one here. She blew out a breath and relaxed against the leather seat as she parked the car.

She opened the car door and gasped as the cold, bitter air smacked her in the face. She fumbled to pull her coat around her with gloved hands. Wishing she had a scarf to protect her neck from the freezing temperatures, her hair whipped across her face and into her eyes.

She pulled the hood of her coat up around her head to

keep out the chill. Then she hurried toward the house and approached the front door, which she found locked. She felt like an idiot for thinking that the door would be unlocked.

She looked around and under everything on the porch but found nothing. No key to unlock the door that she hoped would answer all her questions. But she knew it wouldn't be that easy; nothing falls into your lap when you ask for it. No, it's usually when you least expect it. Yet, she would not give up. She had to know if this girl was real. She had to know about the body she had found and whether something connected them. The two girls at school had said that a girl was missing, and then they were talking about the girl Sara had found last night. So that must mean there was someone else out there. And she wasn't leaving until she found what she was looking for. She just hoped she'd find it here.

She wasn't sure what she was thinking when she came out to this house. Was it answers or a sign pointing in the direction she needed to look? No, she knew that wouldn't happen. She came to find the girl in the pink coat, if she was indeed real. Because seriously, at this point in Sara's mind, she thought she had made the entire scene up. That the rain had somehow created something that resembled a body. She was sure she had seen her, but she had nothing to go on but a necklace and a pink coat. Then it hit her. The girl with auburn hair had said that Megan had left town. But who was Megan besides Officer Rosmus's niece?

She knew what she needed to do now. She needed to find out more about Megan. But who would she ask? Who could she ask? No one knew who Sara was, just the new girl in town, who seemed to appear out of nowhere on a stormy night. Still, someone had to know what was going on here, right? They couldn't all be oblivious to what was happening in this town. She couldn't be the only one who sensed something was off?

Sara walked back down the porch steps. She halted as soon as her feet touched the ground, turning her gaze toward the house. Had she really heard something from inside? She straightened up and slowly turned back around to face the front door. She prayed that her mind wasn't playing the same tricks on her again and that she truly saw a girl standing in the doorway.

Sara scanned the girl up and down until her gaze settled on the girl's leg. Her mouth fell open. She couldn't be? Could she? Sara was afraid to blink, fearful that if she closed her eyes even for a tiny, infinite second, this person in front of her would disappear just like she had the night Sara had seen her on the road.

"Can I help you?" the girl questioned.

Sara could only nod, yet she felt confused. The girl didn't recognize her from that night. How could she not know that she was the one there trying to help her? She had been inches away from her face. Well, in all honesty, it had been raining, and it was hard to see. Even Sara wasn't certain about what she had seen that night. So, yeah, she could understand if the girl didn't recognize her.

"Can we talk?" Sara asked.

The girl glanced around before stepping back into the house. "Come in."

Sara's feet felt heavy as she climbed back up the wooden steps and into the house. The door closed behind her, leaving her in complete darkness with a girl she didn't know. *She could be a serial killer,* Sara thought, then chuckled to herself.

She turned around, but the girl wasn't there. She felt a movement beside her and turned toward it. "*Keep calm,*" she told herself. She blinked, and the girl appeared in front of her, walking away. Sara followed her until they reached the kitchen.

The girl sat at the kitchen table. "Do I know you?"

Sara shook her head.

"Please sit."

Sara pulled out a chair and sat across from the girl. "How is your leg? Do you want me to look at it?" she asked.

"It's not broke. There's just a deep cut, but I have it bandaged," said the girl.

By the looks of her, the girl appeared to be fourteen or fifteen, but Sara wasn't very good at estimating someone's age. These days, girls wore so much makeup that they looked older than they really were, but this girl wasn't wearing any. She looked young and worn out. Then Sara wondered if the girl lived here or was hiding out. She favored the second scenario, as the place was dark and didn't seem lived in. She recalled what had happened to the Tanners, making her shudder at the memory. This girl in front of her didn't live here; this she was sure of. But then, why was she here?

"I'd like to look at your leg. You know, make sure that it's not infected," Sara said. Besides what she had learned in school, she knew little about how to care for a wound, but she felt she had to help this poor girl out.

"Okay," the girl said as she extended her leg to the side.

Sara stood and walked over, sliding the chair she was sitting in to prop the girl's leg up. She pulled the thick fabric of the jeans up and removed the gauze the girl had wrapped around her leg. Sara swallowed as bile rose in the back of her throat. She wasn't good at seeing things like this. The leg looked bad, and she had never seen anything this gross and disgusting in her life. But she couldn't let the girl know this. *Keep your cool,* Sara, she told herself. The girl had an infected leg. *How was it not broken?* Sara seemed to question herself. She knew if she didn't get this girl to the hospital, she would lose her leg.

"Did you put any peroxide on it?" Sara asked.

The girl shook her head.

"I'll go get some and clean it up for you." Sara stood and started walking out of the room, only to stop a few feet away. She had no idea where the bathroom was. "Can you tell me where the bathroom is?"

The girl pointed toward the second floor.

Sara started up the stairs but then stopped. "Will you be here when I get back?"

The girl nodded, appearing confused by Sara's question.

Sara quickly ran up the stairs and to the right. She entered a huge bedroom and went into the bathroom, where she found the first aid kit scattered across the bathroom floor along with bloody towels. She searched through the cabinet, found what she needed, and collected some clean bandages from the floor on her way out. The girl was still sitting in the chair in the kitchen when she came back down the stairs.

Sara cleaned the lesion as best she could and applied some Neosporin along with a clean bandage. "There, that should take care of it for now, but I should take you to a doctor."

The girl shook her head.

Sara looked up at the girl and wondered why she wasn't

talking when she could speak, as she had moments ago.

"Do you live here? What is your name?" Sara asked.

"Abby, and no, I don't live here in this house."

Sara nodded. "Can I call your parents? They're probably worried sick about you." Sara's mind was spinning with every scenario of why this girl didn't just go home and who she was running from. Why was she running? Then, as if she'd forgotten, she remembered why she was here. She couldn't go home either. She had run away, too.

"I can't leave until they catch her," Abby whispered.

Chapter 20

Sara's eyebrows furrowed. “Catch who, Abby?”

“I don’t know her name. I thought she was my best friend, Megan, but Megan wouldn’t have tried to kill me.”

“Kill you?” Sara questioned. “Was that why you were on that road the night I came to town?”

Abby shook her head as if avoiding the question. “It happened here. She hit me over the head with a steel pipe, then I woke up next to a hole in the woods,” Abby said, pointing out the sliding glass doors. “My head was hurting, and there was blood, not a lot, but enough to freak me out. I realized that she wasn’t there, so I started running in the opposite direction,” Abby paused. Her eyes moved side to side as if trying to picture it in her mind. “It all seemed like a blur. I tripped, and that’s when I hurt my leg. I made it to the road when it started pouring down rain. I must have fallen again and lost consciousness because the next thing I saw was darkness around me.” Abby looked away, taking a breath, then spoke again. “I remember little after that. I just remember being back here, in this house. When I saw the police arrive yesterday, I panicked and hid downstairs, but no one came into the house until you. Until today.

Sara absorbed every word Abby said, which all made sense to her. This poor girl was frightened for her life, but Sara didn’t believe she had anything to fear anymore because she was certain this girl who had tried to kill her…

Well, she wasn't quite sure where she was, but she had an idea.

"What does your friend look like? Do you have a picture of her?" Sara asked, still kneeling in front of Abby.

Abby nodded, pulled her cell phone from her pants pocket, and powered it on. She turned the phone toward Sara, causing her to fall back, her tailbone smacking the wooden floor.

"Have you seen her?" Abby asked, looking anxious.

"Yes, I have. I'm afraid that she's… she's dead."

"Dead? Megan's dead? Oh, God. That girl killed her!" Abby shrieked in horror.

"Yesterday, I was taking a walk, and I stumbled across this house. I went into the woods. She was lying inside a hole in the ground. Like someone was about to bury her." Then it hit her. Could it have been the same hole Abby had just mentioned? Yes, she was sure it was. "I'm not sure if it was Megan. Officer Rosmus said a different name."

"What? What did she say?"

"That the girl's name was Robyn."

"Robyn," Abby mumbled, shaking her head. "I don't know anyone named Robyn. You said she looked like her?" Abby questioned, pointing at the photo on her phone.

Sara nodded.

"There has to be some explanation. Do you think she has a twin sister?" Abby asked.

Sara hadn't considered that far ahead because she didn't even know Megan or this Robyn girl.

"And you're sure that she's dead?" Abby questioned, her eyes wide with fear.

"Yes." Sara closed her eyes, wanting to erase the image

from yesterday, but it was too late. She would never forget what that poor girl looked like, even if she had been a murderer. A killer. She was still a person, though Sara didn't know the whole story behind what Abby had said; she couldn't take sides. Then she wondered why she was even thinking about this. This wasn't the time to decide if someone was good or bad. None of this made any sense to her.

Before she could stop herself, the image of the girl in the woods flashed in her mind—the decomposition of the body. The hollow look on the girl stared up at the sky. "A thick root had pierced her back and into her chest, through her heart. That's how I think she died, but Officer Rosmus is doing an autopsy on her." Why had she given Abby such a detailed description of the girl's death? She didn't have to say how the root had punctured her heart.

Abby appeared relieved as the pale skin of her face turned a shade of pink and then almost red. Her shoulders relaxed, and she leaned back against the chair, causing the wooden legs to scrape across the floor.

Abby spoke as if it all registered at once. "You said she looked exactly like my friend, Megan? But you swear that it wasn't Megan, but a girl named Robyn?"

Sara nodded, though she couldn't be certain of the name she thought she heard come from Officer Rosmus's mouth. She stood at least twenty feet away when she muttered the name, but she couldn't tell Abby this. She was frightened enough. She just wished she could prove to Abby that she was safe, but without showing her a picture of the girl she had found, which she didn't have, thank God. Abby would have to believe in what Sara had told her.

"Come on, I'll help you to my car, and I'll take you home. You'll be safe there. No one is coming after you," Sara said.

Tingles pricked the skin of her calf as she stood. Her leg had fallen asleep. She shook her leg to the side, trying to make the sensation of crawling ants disappear before helping Abby to her feet. She thought for sure that the girl would protest about going home, but she didn't.

When Sara opened the front door to the house, it was snowing—not just a few flakes. No, it was coming down fast and hard, but she could still see her car in the distance, wishing she had parked closer to the house. However, she didn't know for sure if she would find anyone here in this house, nor that it would snow.

A few minutes later, Sara had Abby in the front seat and buckled in. She turned the car around and drove away from the Tanner house, hopefully for the last time. By the time Sara pulled up along the curb outside Abby's home, the snow had tapered off. The sky was a solid gray, almost white, but no snow was falling. It was more depressing the longer she thought about it. The sky looked so dull. The sun should be out on a day like today since she had brought this girl home—the girl she had first seen on the road a week ago. The heavens above should glorify her.

Sara glanced at Abby before looking out the windshield, where she noticed a car in the driveway, indicating that someone was home.

"Do you want me to go to the door first, or do you want to go with me?" Sara asked.

Abby looked at Sara and then out the passenger window.

"I'll go with you," Abby replied as she unbuckled her seatbelt.

Sara nodded, opened the car door, and got out. She walked around the rear of the car and opened the passenger door when she heard someone call out.

"Can I help you?" a woman asked.

Sara turned toward the woman standing in the doorway, then turned back to Abby and helped her out of the car. Abby stood facing the house when Sara heard the woman, whom she was certain was Abby's mother. The woman cried out in shock. Or was it excitement? She wasn't sure, but the woman seemed ecstatic to see her daughter again. The woman was beside them in seconds, knocking Sara out of the way to hug her daughter.

"Oh, my God, where have you been? Are you alright? Are you hurt? Oh, my God, Abby. I've been so worried about you." "Your father and I have been looking for you," the woman said as she pulled Abby away, yet held her at arm's length, searching over her face.

"I'm okay, Mom, really I am. Thanks to this girl," Abby said, looking over at Sara and smiling.

Sara didn't know what to say. She was just glad the girl was okay and that she was safe and alive. This past week, she had thought she was losing her mind. She had thought she imagined this girl lying in the road, but now she knew she hadn't.

"Wait, before you go, I have something for you," Sara said as she ducked back into the car and came out holding the half-heart necklace. "This belongs to you."

Abby's eyes narrowed when she saw the necklace that Sara held in her hand before touching one hand to the base of her neck. She looked down at her palm, which held a necklace with the opposite words. "That's not my necklace? I have mine," Abby said, showing Sara the half-hearted necklace from around her neck.

Sara looked at her in confusion. Maybe her friend had lost the necklace, but that wouldn't explain how it had ended up on the road unless Abby had it with her. But she would have said she had lost her friend's necklace, which she hadn't said.

Should she ask her? No, she didn't want to delve into how she had found the necklace, although she knew someone would eventually ask her questions. Like how she knew that Abby was at the Tanner house? Where did she find the necklace? She was just glad that the girl was alive and now home with her family, that this whole mess was finally over. Though deep inside, she knew it was just the beginning.

Chapter 21

When Sara woke the next morning, she wasn't expecting to be the talk of the town. She didn't want the publicity. She wanted nothing more than to hide out in the house she was now calling home and live a quiet life. But she should have known that when she took Abby home yesterday, the news would spread quickly, like wildfire.

Just as she was leaving for school, there was a knock on the door. She had assumed it would be Mick because they had been driving to school together. When she opened the door, she found a uniformed police officer standing on the porch.

"Good morning. Sara, is it?" Officer Rosmus asked.

Sara only nodded. She was afraid to speak as a knot formed in her stomach, and her throat tightened. She did not understand why she felt paranoid. She had done nothing wrong but find a dead body in the woods. Then she went back to the same house and found Abby. So why was the police officer here? Her stomach twisted, threatening to eject the breakfast she had just eaten. Did she discover who she was and plan to take her back to her real home?

"May I come in?"

Her feet were planted firmly where she stood. But she knew she would eventually have to answer the questions Officer Rosmus was here to ask, wouldn't she? Did she have the right to ***refuse to*** answer any of her questions? She was the victim, though no crime had been committed. It wasn't about whether she had done anything wrong; it was about being sent back to where she had come from. She didn't want this officer running a background check on her because she knew that then she would have to get in her car and drive away from this town. She would have to leave Edith and Mick behind. But she didn't want to leave. So, what was she going to do? That was the million-dollar question.

"May I come in?" Officer Crystal Rosmus asked again.

Although she didn't want to let this woman into the house, the one where she felt safe, she didn't think she had any other choice. She stepped back and to the side. Once the officer was inside, Sara closed the door.

"Sara, why are you still here?" Edith asked as she entered the room. "Oh, Crystal, it's good to see you. How have you been?"

"I'm good, Ed, and you?"

"Can't complain now that this sweet girl is staying with me. She's been a great help around here." Edith smiled. "Is there something I can help you with?"

"I'm here to speak with Sara."

"Sara?" Edith questioned. "Why do you need to speak with her? Did something happen at school?"

Officer Rosmus looked from Edith to Sara and then back to Edith. "Nothing at school. Sara was the one who found the girl in the woods two days ago and brought the missing girl, Abby, home yesterday. I have more questions for her, that's all."

"Oh? I hadn't known Abby was missing?" Edith questioned. "Does Sara need a lawyer?"

"Well, I don't think she does." Officer Rosmus turned her eyes from Edith back toward Sara. "Do you need a lawyer?"

"What? I did nothing wrong but stumble across that girl I found in the woods. I didn't kill her, as I'm sure the coroner will tell you," Sara replied defensively. She couldn't stop the words from tumbling out of her. She needed to regain control of herself. Was this officer accusing her of killing someone, something she could never do? She wasn't a murderer. A killer. "I'm not sure how I came across finding Abby; it's like, well, I don't know how I knew she was out there in that house." Sara didn't know how much she should tell the officer, but what did it matter? She had nothing to hide, except for her own identity.

"I didn't say that you did anything wrong, or that you killed that girl unless there's something you're not telling me. Is there something you're not telling me?" Rosmus questioned, her eyes were like daggers as if searching for a soul.

Sara shook her head. "No! No, I'm not implying that I had." Sara suddenly felt exhausted. She was a manipulator. Skilled at twisting her words and making her feel as if she were the guilty one, but she wasn't guilty. She was innocent. That wasn't even a question or a thought that should have crossed her mind. **She. Had. Done. Nothing. Wrong.**

"Good, now that we have that settled, let's get to the reason I'm here," Officer Rosmus said.

"Come, we'll sit at the kitchen table. Do you want some coffee, Crystal?" Edith asked.

"That sounds wonderful," Officer Rosmus replied. "It's a bit nippy out there this morning. I heard that it may drop to a negative twenty-five-degree wind chill later this evening."

Edith nodded, then turned and headed into the kitchen

with Officer Rosmus following closely behind.

Sara stayed behind as she watched Officer Rosmus follow Edith into the kitchen. Her mind was reeling with inquiries. Did this officer think she had something to do with what had happened in this town? She had arrived a week ago, which, according to her recollection, was the same night she had seen the body in the road. That was also when this other girl died in the woods, but she didn't know for sure if that was when the girl had died. Besides, she was nowhere near that area in the woods. But how could she prove this to the police? She couldn't. All she had was Abby's word, even though Abby claimed that she was unconscious when Sara had found her on the road. Or had she heard her wrong? Her mind was a train wreck. Her thinking had been off-kilter since she had left Bristol. Now she was back to square one. It was her word against Abby's.

Sara took a deep breath and then exhaled. Well, she had nothing to worry about. She did nothing wrong. That was the truth. Why was she even questioning herself? If she kept this up, they would haul her off to a psychiatric ward for an evaluation. Maybe this town was just like Wayward Pines, like on TV, and she had made a grave mistake turning onto the road that night and entering this small, creepy town. One that she may never leave alive.

"Sara," Edith hollered from inside the kitchen. "Are you coming?"

Sara shook the thoughts from her head and walked into the kitchen just as Edith poured Officer Rosmus a cup of coffee.

"Sara, do you want a cup?" Edith asked.

Sara shook her head. She wasn't sure she could swallow

the hot liquid for fear of the coffee coming back up. She just wanted this conversation to end so she could move on with the rest of her pathetic life. Sara sat down next to Edith, wishing to be as far away from Officer Rosmus as possible.

"So, tell me what night you arrived in Craven Falls?" Rosmus asked.

"About a week ago," Sara replied, chewing the inside of her lip and tasting blood.

"About a week ago? Do you know the day?" Rosmus asked. "I like to get the facts straight."

"It was late Sunday night," Sara replied. A night she would never forget.

"So, a little over a week then? About ten days, to be exact?"

Sara nodded. She couldn't believe how particular this officer was being toward her.

"And what brought you here on a late Sunday night?" Rosmus asked. "As it seems, you weren't just stopping to rest for the night."

Sara's stomach clenched into a tight ball. She was becoming furious with this woman and all her questions. What did it matter to her why Sara was driving around late in the pouring rain on a freaking Sunday night? What difference did it make? Sara didn't need to look up at the officer because she could feel her eyes glaring at her. She needed to tell her something believable.

"I got kicked out of my mom's house, so I got in the car and drove. I didn't know until I turned onto the road that I would be here in the town of Craven Falls. It just happened," Sara said. "Just like everything else that was happening. It all just happened. I wasn't looking for it or did any of it."

Sara's voice rose. She wasn't sure where all this anger was coming from, and she couldn't stop it now that it had started. She felt a hand touch her right arm, and she closed her mouth, sealing off any further words from escaping. She didn't want to look up. She didn't want to make eye contact with either woman sitting at the table.

"Okay, so something made you go out to the Tanner house and into the woods. And that's when you found the body? And then yesterday, you went back out to the same house and found Abby, who has been missing since the night you arrived? And was this the first time you have seen Abby?" Rosmus asked.

"Yes, I went for a walk and ended up at that house. I can't explain why or how I ended up in the woods where I had found that dead girl. And as for Abby, I saw her on the road the night I arrived," Sara said, looking from Edith to Officer Rosmus. "I went to help her, but when I turned around after doing something in my car, she had disappeared. It was pouring down rain. I didn't know where she had gone, so I got back into my car and kept on driving until I saw the Bed and Breakfast sign out on the street." She wasn't sure why she had just told them about that night. She hadn't meant to, but it was out there now.

Officer Rosmus nodded while writing in her notebook.

"The girl I found in the woods. What was her name?"

Officer Rosmus didn't lift her head when she spoke. "Her name was Robyn Wilde."

"Abby said she looked just like her best friend Megan. Is that true?"

"I don't know anything about that. I guess they looked similar, but no relation to one another," Rosmus replied.

If Sara had learned one thing from her past with Brad, it was that Officer Rosmus was lying.

Chapter 22

A minute after Officer Rosmus left the house, Mick arrived. Sara grabbed her things and hurried out the door without saying goodbye to Edith. She no longer wanted to be inside the house, not after the officer had sat there accusing her of something she didn't understand. The more Sara reflected on the conversation with the officer, the more she realized that perhaps she was the one accusing herself of the crime.

As she drove to school, Sara kept to herself and let Mick do all the talking, but that wasn't anything new for any other day. Mick seemed to enjoy talking. Maybe she was lonely and had no one at home to converse with. Did it matter? Not really; Sara didn't care as she had other things on her mind right now.

Sara wasn't sure how she knew that Officer Rosmus was lying. She could tell by the lack of eye contact. The officer had kept her head down the entire conversation, writing in that stupid notepad of hers. Now she just had to find out why she was lying, and what she was hiding. Who was that girl she had found dead in the woods, and how was she related to this Megan girl? Sara was certain there was a connection between the two. Officer Rosmus claimed there was no relation, which was bullpucky. It was apparent there was a connection, a similarity between the two. Why would Officer Rosmus cover up the truth? Mick had said that Megan was Officer Rosmus' niece, which would mean this

Robyn girl was her niece as well? The question that now occupied her thoughts was: where was this Megan girl, and why did she and her mother leave so quickly?

With everything swirling in her mind, Sara hadn't realized that she had gotten out of her car and was now inside the school. She felt comatose. She hadn't even remembered parting ways with Mick or that she was standing at her locker. Looking around, she found Mick was nowhere in sight.

"Get it together," she mumbled under her breath.

She entered her combination, opened her locker, took the books she needed, and walked down the hallway. The two girls from yesterday were standing at their lockers. The same two girls she had overheard discussing Megan. Should she approach them and ask about her? Find out where she might have gone?

All she wanted was to solve this little mystery about the photo Abby had shown her. The two girls looked identical. Megan and this Robyn Wilde girl, whom Officer Rosmus said weren't related. "Bullshit," she whispered. Before she could stop herself, she strutted up to the girl with brown hair and braces whom she had seen yesterday.

"Excuse me, I couldn't help but hear you talking yesterday about a girl named Megan?" Sara interrupted.

"I'm sorry, do we know you?" asked the brunette with braces.

"I just arrived here last week and overheard you talking about a girl named Megan. She was friends with Abby.

The two girls exchanged glances before turning back to Sara.

"Wait, are you the one who found Abby and brought her home yesterday?" asked the other girl with auburn hair.

Sara nodded.

"How did you find her? Did you know she was staying out at the Tanner house?" the brunette inquired.

"Dumb luck, I guess," Sara replied, smiling brightly.

The two girls, who seemed engrossed in Sara's story, nodded simultaneously.

"Were you also the one who found that body in the woods, too?" the brunette girl asked.

Sara swallowed. She felt as though she were being interrogated by the two tenth graders. Before she knew it, a crowd had gathered around them. She felt nervous. She hated being the center of attention.

"Yes, I was the one who found her."

"What did she look like?" asked the girl with auburn hair.

"Aubrey, why would you ask that question?" the brunette shouted.

"I'm sorry, Elly, but it's… It's just that it all seems coincidental to me. She arrived here last week and now she has found a dead body, and Abby," Aubrey said to her friend Elly.

"Well, I don't believe she had anything to do with either of them," Elly replied.

Sara couldn't believe that the two girls were fighting about this. And no, she had nothing to do with either of the two girls she had stumbled upon. Why did everyone think she did? Just because she was the new girl in town. Well, that was cat shit on a stick.

The bell rang, and Sara stepped back, now swallowed by

the crowd of students listening in on the conversation—a conversation she was no longer part of. She slipped away from the growing crowd as the two girls continued to bicker and made her way to class across the hall. She had gotten nowhere with those two girls. Maybe she would ask them later after school, when no one else was around, if they didn't start arguing again.

+ + +

When school was over, Sara closed her locker door and headed outside toward her car on the other side of the student parking lot. She spotted a police cruiser driving slowly through the rows of parked cars as if looking for something or someone. She stopped in her tracks and watched as the police cruiser stopped behind her car and seemed to run her plates.

"Shit," Sara swore. The police were now investigating her background. She knew they would eventually, but she had hoped for more time. It had to be Officer Rosmus; she was sure of this. Rosmus had sent a cop to run her plates and gather more information about her.

A minute later, the police car moved along and stopped at another vehicle several cars down from hers to check their plates. *Who were they looking for, if not her?* She questioned herself.

Students rushed out the doors, down the front steps, and around where Sara stood on the sidewalk in front of the school.

"Hey, do you still have questions about Megan?" said a voice from behind her.

Sara turned and saw that it was Aubrey from this morning. She looked around but didn't see her friend Elly with her.

"Yes," Sara said, nodding.

"Come with me. We'll talk over there," Aubrey pointed to a tree next to the school.

Sara walked behind Aubrey along the sidewalk, distancing themselves from their classmates.

"My grandfather is the sheriff here in Craven Falls. Sheriff White. I was getting something from the fridge last night and overheard him talking to someone on the phone. I don't know who it was, but he said that Megan had a twin sister."

"Robyn," Sara whispered.

"Yes, how did you know her name?" Aubrey asked.

Sara wasn't sure how much to tell Aubrey. She hardly knew her; in fact, she didn't know her at all. But what did she have to lose? She wasn't hiding anything. She just wanted the truth. The only way she would get the truth was by asking questions and telling Aubrey what she knew, without giving too much detail.

"Officer Rosmus was at my house this morning, and she said that the body I found belonged to a Robyn Wilde."

"Robyn Wilde? Who is that?" Aubrey questioned. "Do you think they're twins? No one here, as far as I know, knew Megan had a sister, especially a twin sister."

Sara shrugged her shoulders. "Your guess is as good as mine. I don't know anyone here, except Mick and Edith. I wasn't looking to come here and solve some mystery."

"So, why are you here? Someone said you ran away from home.

Sara stiffened. How in the hell did this rumor spread so fast? Well, it wasn't a rumor, but… then it hit her. She had told Officer Rosmus that she and her mom had a fight and that she left. That's how she ended up in this town. She should have known that word would get around here. She just didn't think it would happen so quickly. She had just talked to Officer Rosmus that morning at Edith's house, and now this girl, Aubrey, knew about it, which meant everyone else did too.

"Yes, I did, but that has nothing to do with this Robyn girl and Abby. It's all just coincidental. I had nothing to do with either of them. I don't even know them," Sara replied.

They both stood there beneath the maple tree, neither saying a word. What was there to say when so many questions still needed answers?

Chapter 23

When Aubrey and Sara finished talking, they went their separate ways, which left Sara with more questions than answers—answers she had to find. It was like the calm before the storm; she just didn't know what would happen next. As she walked away, it dawned on her that Aubrey had been wearing a black winter coat. Could it have been her I had seen outside the library? She turned around, scanning the scenery, but the girl was gone.

When Sara arrived at her car, the only one left in the parking lot, she saw Mick sitting at the curb beside the driver's side.

"Hey, there you are," Mick said. "I was looking for you but couldn't find you anywhere. I knew you were still here because, duh, your car is here," Mick laughed at herself.

Sara smiled. "Yeah, sorry, I was just talking to a girl I had met this morning. My God, you must be freezing?"

Mick seemed to nod at her answer. "Yeah, but it's okay. It's no problem. Are you ready to go? I have to be at work in ten minutes."

"Yep, I'm ready," Sara replied. "Is your boss hiring? I could use a job. You know, make some money."

Mick smiled. "Really? I'll ask him when I get to work. You should come in and introduce yourself. Let him talk to you."

Sara nodded. "Okay, yeah. Sounds good."

A few minutes later, Sara pulled up along the sidewalk in front of the café just as the heat poured out of the vent. Both Sara and Mick seemed to shudder at the same moment, filling the car with laughter, neither wanting to get out into the freezing cold.

* * *

"So, when can you start?" Mr. Waters asked.

"Really?" Sara questioned excitedly.

"I'm assuming you would work evenings along with Mick and weekends too?"

"Yes, that would be great. I can start tomorrow. Right after school," Sara said.

"Great. Here are some forms to fill out. You can bring them with you tomorrow when your shift starts at 3:00 p.m."

Sara nodded. "Thank you so much, Mr. Waters."

Sara stopped to chat with Mick before leaving the café, informing her that she got the job and would see her in the morning.

As Sara drove down the street and turned into the driveway of the Bed and Breakfast, she realized that she wouldn't need to drive to work since it would only take her a couple of minutes to walk. That also depended on the weather.

Once she parked the car in the garage, she entered the house through the back door by the kitchen. She heard Edith talking to someone, but it wasn't on the phone since it was still hanging on the wall in the kitchen. The person was somewhere in the house. Sara paused just inside the kitchen doorway and glanced around the corner, but she couldn't see the person with Edith. The person sitting in the other chair was out of sight from the kitchen.

"How long will you be in town this time?" Edith asked.

"Oh, not long. Maybe one. Two nights at the most," said the male voice.

Edith said, "Well, I will show you to your room, and then if you're hungry, I can make you something to eat."

"That would be great," the man said.

Sara stepped back into the kitchen until the two of them had gone up the stairs. She wasn't sure what she was afraid of. She hadn't recognized the voice. It didn't sound like Brad's, but she couldn't be certain. Didn't all men sound somewhat alike? No. She knew that they didn't all sound the same. She was just being paranoid. Brad wasn't in town.

Chapter 24

Sara opened her eyes and looked at the clock on the nightstand. "Shit!" she shouted as she jumped out from under the warm comfort of her blankets and sprang to her feet. She was sure she had set the alarm, but it hadn't gone off. She would be late for school.

She grabbed some clean clothes and hurried out of the bedroom. Just as she entered the hall, she ran right into the chest of a man. The same man who was staying here at the Bed and Breakfast.

"I'm so sorry," Sara said as she stepped back away from him. "I didn't mean to… I'm just running late, is all."

The man held his arms out, placing them on either side of Sara's as if to prevent her from falling over, even though she wasn't. She had been startled by the sudden stop she made right into the chest of this muscular man. Embarrassment washed over her, and she felt ashamed for being so careless and in such a hurry.

"It's fine," the man said with a deep chuckle. "There's nothing to apologize for."

Sara looked up into the man's eyes. This was the first time they had met since he arrived here yesterday. He had gone into the room that Edith had given him and hadn't come out until now. Had he been so exhausted that he slept through the entire day and night? She had to believe this was true because she had nothing else to go on. She hadn't seen him at dinner last night or before going to bed herself.

She took another step back from the man. His arms dropped to his sides, releasing her from his hold. This gave Sara a better view of him. He was tall, maybe six feet, with a laugh that made her insides flutter. He had sandy blond hair and blue-green eyes like the sea that Sara had seen in many pictures on the internet. The waters of Jamaica, where you could see all the way to the bottom, whether you were standing on the beach or looking down from an airplane. These were eyes you could get lost in, just as she was at that very moment.

"Are you okay?" he asked.

When she realized that she was staring at this gorgeous man in front of her, her eyes dropped to the floor. "I'm sorry, but I have to go get ready," she said and hurried past him and into the bathroom, closing the door behind her.

She rested her back against the door, exhaling the breath she hadn't known she was holding. She turned and looked in the mirror to her left. Her face was flushed. Was she blushing from the touch of this man she knew nothing about? She hadn't realized that a total stranger could have this much power over someone like he had over her seconds ago.

From the looks of him, she would say he seemed to be in his late twenties. But what did it matter how old he was? She wasn't interested in him, and besides, he was only here for a day or two, according to Edith. So why was she getting all hot and bothered by this man? This she didn't know and didn't want to figure out. She wasn't here to meet anyone. No, she was here to escape from one, not to start a new relationship. Besides, he was leaving.

* * *

Fifteen minutes later, she bounded down the stairs just as

someone knocked on the front door.

"I'll get it," Sara hollered as she stepped off the last step. She moved aside the curtain that hung over the small window across from the door and saw Mick standing on the porch. Sara opened the door, and frigid air blew onto her face. She turned away to shield herself from the cold.

Mick slipped past her, and Sara shut the door.

"Oh, my God, it's so freaking cold out there," Mick said, her teeth chattering. "I can't believe we're still having school today. I think my phone said it's a -20° wind chill outside."

"And that's why I said I would pick you up at your place, so you don't have to walk," Sara said.

Mick stood silent as if Sara had said nothing.

"Well, okay then, I guess I'll go start the car and let it warm up before we leave," Sara said and walked away. She cut through the kitchen and out the back door to her car. After starting her car, she headed back inside to keep warm with Mick and Edith before they left for school.

Sara poured herself a cup of coffee and picked a banana from the bowl on the counter.

"You don't want me to make you anything?" Edith asked.

"No, I don't have time today. My alarm didn't go off, and I had to rush this morning. This will be fine, but thank you for asking," Sara replied.

"No problem, maybe Steve will want something to eat before he gets back on the road today, that's if he's leaving," Edith said.

She seemed confused at first, but then it clicked that she was talking about the man upstairs. Sara nodded as flashes of this Steve guy she knew nothing about flickered through her head: his bulging muscles and sea-blue-green eyes. She couldn't forget how amazing his smile was or his deep voice.

"Are you okay?" Mick asked.

Sara looked up at Mick. "Yes, why?"

"Your cheeks are red. Are you feeling alright?"

"Yes, I'm fine," Sara retorted. "I'm sorry. I didn't mean to snap at you. We should go. The car should be warm by now." Sara felt flustered.

"But it's only been five minutes, there's no way it's heated by now," Mick said.

Sara just wanted to leave the house before Steve came down from upstairs. She couldn't risk seeing him again. Why was she acting this way? She wasn't sure. She didn't even know this guy. She had seen him for the first time that morning, yet she acted as if they had gone out on a date or had a one-night stand, trying to avoid him.

She shook her head as she walked toward the coatrack. She slipped into the boots sitting by the back door and zipped up her coat. She pulled the hood over her head and snapped it into place, tying the scarf she found around her neck.

Several minutes later, they sat in the warm Eldorado, driving down the driveway. Before turning onto the street, Sara glanced into the rearview mirror facing the Bed and Breakfast. The man from this morning, Steve, watched her from the bedroom window of his room.

Sara felt a sense of uneasiness at that moment. Was he watching her? Was he here to find her? This, she didn't know, but she prayed that wasn't true. She had never seen him before this morning, had she? No, she was sure she hadn't. Her mind flicked through the images of all Brad's guy friends. Nope, this man's face wasn't one of them. She was positive.

She snapped out of her thoughts, taking her eyes off the rearview mirror and turning right onto the main street that ran through Craven Falls.

If she had looked across the street to her left, which she hadn't when she pulled out of the driveway, she might have noticed a man sitting in a car parked on the street across from the Bed and Breakfast.

Chapter 25

After school, Sara drove to the café with Mick. She parked the car in the employee-only back parking lot, which would be unseen by anyone driving by. Not that she thought anyone would look for her car, but in the back of her mind, she still knew Brad was out there, and hiding in this small town was just temporary. She could feel it in her bones: an uneasiness crept along her skin.

Although school was canceled for the rest of the week due to temperatures dropping well below zero, Sara still had to work, which she was fine with. She needed something to keep herself and her mind busy since there was nothing else to do.

She looked up as the bell above the café door *dinged* and Officer Rosmus marched in. Sara hadn't realized until now how loud the woman entered a room. Confused about why she was stomping her boots when there was no snow outside, Sara wasn't the only one who looked toward the door, as the noise the officer was making made everyone's head turn and glare.

Sara locked eyes with Officer Rosmus as she wiped the crumbs away with a warm, soapy rag. She hoped the officer wasn't there to question her. She was working and didn't have time for the officer's cross-examination. She was just in the wrong place at the wrong time, or was it the wrong place at the right time? Considering she had found a dead body and then Abby, who had apparently *been* missing. Yet, no one *had been* searching for her because, according to the rumors around town, no one even knew she was missing. At least she hadn't heard of anyone looking for Abby. But what did it matter now? The girl was home safe and with her family.

Sara didn't want to even think about the girl she had found in the woods, nor about Abby, whom she hadn't seen since she had taken her home. At that moment, she wondered whether the girl's leg was better. Had her parents taken her to the hospital to have it checked and treated? This she didn't know, but she could always stop by and see her—to check on her. Would doing so bring more questions onto her plate? Again, she had nothing to do with the terrible things going on in this town, but apparently, the people here didn't see it that way. All they saw was an outsider who came into town, and bad things started happening. Her mind recalled the articles she had read at the library.

No.

Bad things had happened here long before she arrived in Craven Falls. They just wanted someone to blame.

Officer Rosmus walked toward the counter and took a seat on one of the bar stools next to a man with short, black, wavy hair. "Hey, Reece, how is the store these days?" Rosmus asked.

Reece, who was chewing, washed the food down with some coffee before replying. "It's good. Not so busy right now with the weather, but we're still open just like the café."

Sara placed the washcloth in the bucket under the counter. "What can I get for you, Officer?" Sara asked, not wanting to make eye contact again.

"Just coffee is fine. Thank you," Officer Rosmus said.

Sara nodded, turned around, picked up the pot of hot, freshly brewed coffee, and poured some into a cup.

Sara asked Reece, now that she knew his name, "Would you like more?"

He nodded. "Thank you."

When Sara finished, she took the pot of coffee and walked around the counter to the tables where people were sitting. She was heading back behind the counter when she heard the familiar sound of the bell ringing above the door. She turned to greet whoever had entered. The pot dropped from her hand and crashed to the floor, sending hot liquid flying in all directions along with shattered glass.

Both Officer Rosmus and Reece turned at the sound of glass breaking, yet no one moved from their seats to help her.

Sara seemed unconcerned about them, the coffee, or the broken glass scattered across the linoleum floor. She fixed her gaze on the man who had just entered the café through the door.

Sara looked away and dropped to the floor, wiping the fragments of glass and coffee into a pile with the rag she had in the drawstring of her apron. Her hands were shaking. Hell, her whole body trembled with fear, but she wasn't sure why. It was as if she feared this person she didn't know and had only met for the first time this morning. Earlier, she had flutters in her stomach, and now she felt scared. Frightened of this man, but she didn't know why. Was it because she had seen him watching her from the bedroom window this morning? She didn't know.

"Are you alright, Miss?" Steve asked.

Sara looked up just as Steve, the man staying at the Bed and Breakfast, knelt down to help her.

Sara nodded. She felt mute, like a mime. What was wrong with her? She was sure that her reaction would certainly raise more questions for Officer Rosmus now, given the way she was acting around this man she didn't know.

Mick appeared beside her to help wipe up the mess. "Sara, are you okay? You didn't get cut, did you?" Mick asked.

Sara shook her head. "No, I'm fine. I don't know what happened. I just dropped it, I guess."

"It's not the first time this has happened. We have more pots in the back," Mick said.

"Okay, thanks," Sara replied. She turned and scooped up the rest of the glass onto the tray that Mick had brought her before standing. When she turned back around, Steve was gone. Relief swept over her until she looked around and spotted him sitting in a booth, facing the other way, away from her.

Sara carried the tray of broken glass and soaked towels to the kitchen. When she finished, she asked if she could take a short break to regain her composure before returning to work. She entered the restroom and locked the door. Staring into the mirror at her reflection, she asked, "What is wrong with me?" although there was no reply. And why would there be? She was talking to herself, not an actual person. She wasn't sure if she was waiting for herself to answer the question, which would confirm that she was losing her mind. She didn't understand what had happened out there. The man wasn't Brad, so why was she acting so weird and nervous around him? She needed to get a hold of herself. Besides, she didn't want to lose her job after the first day. Or, should she say, the first two hours?

There was a soft knock on the door. "Sara, can I come in?" Mick asked.

Sara reached over and unlocked the door. The bathroom wasn't large by any means; perhaps it was the size of a large walk-in closet.

The door opened, and Mick slipped inside, closing the door behind her. "Are you sure you're okay? Mr. Waters said you can go home if you want; besides, we're not that busy. I can handle the customers."

Sara shook her head. "No, I'm fine. I don't need to go home."

Mick nodded. "So, can you tell me what happened out there? Who is that guy?"

Sara shrugged her shoulders. "I don't know who he is. He's staying at the Bed and Breakfast. Came in yesterday, and I ran into him this morning before school. All I know is that his name is Steve," Sara said.

"Well, there's something going on between the two of you," Mick whispered, a hint of a smile playing on her lips.

Sara's eyebrows shot up. "Why would you say that? And why are you smiling?"

"Look, I mean nothing by what I said, but you're acting weird around that guy, so there must be something going on?"

"Well, there isn't, Mick!" Sara shouted.

Mick stepped back, her body pressing against the door of the cramped bathroom.

Sara's shoulders drooped. "I'm sorry. Maybe you're right. I'll just go home for the day and come back tomorrow."

Mick nodded in agreement, turned, opened the door, and slithered through the opening like a snake, leaving Sara alone once again.

She didn't know what was wrong with her, but she needed to get a grip on things. If she thought people were talking about her now, she was giving them more to whisper about behind her back. Brad would not find her here in this town. And as for Steve, well, she didn't know what she would do about him. Besides, he wasn't staying here much longer, according to Edith.

Chapter 26

After returning home, Sara told Edith that she wasn't feeling well and went to her room for the night. She didn't run into Steve, which was a good thing for her. Maybe he had finally left? But she wouldn't know until morning because she wasn't leaving her room unless there was a fire.

She lay under the comfort of the blankets, her mind drifting off to sleep, only to wake several minutes later to the sound of floorboards creaking outside her bedroom door. Her eyes shot open, and she turned her head toward the door. She saw a silhouette through the gap under the door. Someone was standing on the other side of her closed bedroom door.

She lay perfectly still, watching like a scared kitten. Whoever was on the other side of the door didn't move. She knew if it was Edith, she'd knock on the door, wouldn't she? So that only left Steve, who must still be here. But why? There was nothing keeping him here—no huge businesses that were work-related, not that she knew of. So, the question remained: why was this man, Steve, even in this town? Unless… unless he was here for her? Then that would mean Brad sent him? But that wouldn't make any sense because why would he do that? She knew he wouldn't. He'd want to come and get her himself and drag her back, kicking and screaming.

Or maybe Steve ended up here in this town the same way she had? Perhaps it was just coincidence as well? He turned onto the road and continued driving until he arrived in this town, just as she had. There was no other explanation for why he was here, right? Or was she merely trying to invent reasons for why he had come here?

The floorboards creaked again as the shadow moved away from the door, and all she saw was light streaming under the door. The person had left, but why were they even standing outside her door? Was it Steve? Did he know her? Had they met before? This, she knew, wasn't true. She had never seen him in her life. She was certain that if it were Brad, he would simply barge in and kill her, wouldn't he?

She exhaled deeply and closed her eyes, only to open them once more. The light she had seen under the door vanished as the person turned off the hall light. She was sure she wouldn't be sleeping anytime soon.

* * *

Sara opened her eyes and looked at the clock beside the bed. It was after nine in the morning. She wasn't sure when she had fallen asleep, but she had. She felt rested from the previous day's events that had her blood pumping through her veins, making her nervous and afraid.

She rolled onto her back and looked up at the ceiling. Had she been worried for no reason? Was her mind just tired? Exhausted by all the incidents that had occurred since her arrival in Craven Falls? She knew that if she could, she'd rewind time and never have turned onto the road that had led her here to Craven Falls. Even though that meant she would have never met Edith or Mick, it also meant she would have never stumbled across finding Abby and bringing her home, and let's not forget the body of Robyn she had found in the woods. Or maybe she could rewind time and never have gone out with Brad. Yes, that would have changed everything completely, and she would still be at home with her friends. With her grandmother.

She wanted to shut off her brain for once and forget all that had happened. She tossed the covers aside and slid out of bed. She slipped her feet into the slippers, grabbed the robe lying at the foot of the bed, and padded down the hall to the bathroom. She hadn't run into Steve this time and felt immensely relieved. *Maybe he had left and gone on his way, wherever that may be,* Sara thought, allowing her shoulders to relax.

Wrapping the robe around her, she opened the bathroom door and headed downstairs. All she wanted was a hot cup of coffee, and she hoped that Edith had brewed some.

Sara stepped off the last step.

The house was quiet—too quiet, since she usually heard Edith in the kitchen.

She headed toward the kitchen and found it empty. Maybe Edith was still in bed, resting? Yes, she was sure of this because Edith sometimes slept in, especially if she had trouble sleeping the night before.

Sara prepared the coffee, and as it brewed, she padded across the foyer to Edith's bedroom. Upon arriving outside the bedroom, she noticed the door was ajar. The absence of light from inside indicated that Edith was still sleeping and that the blinds were closed.

The hinges squeaked as she pushed the door open, the light from the hall illuminating the room. She saw something, or someone, lying on the bed.

Sara stepped inside, feeling like an intruder. This was Edith's bedroom—her sanctuary where she rested and kept all her belongings that meant everything to her. Sara felt as if she was invading her privacy, her space. She wondered if she should turn around, leave, and close the door as if she hadn't entered at all. But her mind was curious and wanted to ensure that her dear friend Edith was okay.

Although she felt it was sinful to go into Edith's room, she sensed something was wrong. She remembered feeling the same way when she stumbled upon the body in the road, then in the woods, and when she found Abby at that house.

She closed her eyes, something she'd been doing a lot lately, and blew out a breath before walking further into the room. She listened for Edith's breathing but heard nothing, which didn't mean there was anything amiss. Her grandmother was a silent breather, and many times Sara had thought she had died in her sleep, but she hadn't.

Please let her be alive, she thought as she moved further into the room. Sara stood beside the bed and reached out her right hand. She touched Edith's arm, but she didn't stir.

"Edith, are you awake?" Sara whispered, then felt stupid because if Edith were awake, she would have heard her and said something when Sara walked into the room, but she hadn't said anything. She hadn't moved. She hadn't felt Sara lay a hand on her body.

"Edith," Sara spoke again, gently shaking Edith's body this time.

Still nothing.

Something was very, very wrong.

Chapter 27

Sara moved away from the bed and went to the window. She pushed the curtains aside to let in more light. When she turned back around, she noticed a mound of blankets on the bed. She couldn't see Edith's face, which was hidden under a blanket.

Panic bubbled in the furthest point of her stomach. Heat rose through her gut and into her chest, making her feel as if she were on fire. She was literally sweating, yet at the same time, chills coursed through her body—a sensation she felt right before she would vomit.

"God, please don't let her be dead," Sara whispered. Though she wasn't sure why she would automatically think this.

She walked back to the side of the bed, and with a hesitant hand, she moved the top blanket away, like she was peeling an orange. She saw Edith's face. Her eyes were closed, and her skin was pale, but that wasn't anything different. Sara recalled the first night she had arrived here and how pale Edith had looked that evening. In fact, Edith had looked paler every day since Sara had been in this house.

She took a deep breath and held it as she moved her trembling hand toward Edith's neck. Her eyes shifted to the pillow next to Edith's face, which lay askew as if someone had tossed it there.

The breath hissed out of her lungs like a deflating tire.

She didn't want to know if ... Sara couldn't finish the thought, scattering about in her mind. The words sat on her tongue. Yet the thought emerged anyway; she wouldn't be able to handle it if Edith were dead, especially if someone had killed her.

Well, she knew that the thought only entered her mind because of how the pillow lay askew on the bed. Otherwise, she wouldn't have thought such a thing, right? Maybe, maybe not.

Her hand froze mid-air, inches from Edith's face. She watched as her hand trembled. The room wasn't cold. Her teeth weren't chattering. In fact, it was warmer inside than when she was standing in the hall.

Without wasting another second, she placed two fingers against Edith's neck.

Unlike the night she arrived in Craven Falls, when she found the body in the road and felt a pulse on the girl's neck.

She couldn't detect a pulse on Edith's neck.

* * *

Thirty minutes later, Officer Rosmus was standing at the front door, knocking. The house seemed empty as the sounds echoed throughout, bouncing off the painted walls and furnished rooms. Rosmus would have arrived at the house sooner if Sara had called her, but Sara had hesitated after finding Edith unresponsive. It wasn't that she hadn't thought about calling the officer; she had. Rather, she wanted time to say goodbye to the sweet, kind, old lady who had welcomed her into her home when she didn't have to. This lady had also somehow obtained forged transcripts for Sara, enabling her to attend school without the institution discovering that she had run away from home.

Sara opened the front door and led Officer Rosmus to Edith's bedroom. Sara had called the police, informing them that Edith had passed away in her sleep. She had only omitted that she believed someone had murdered Edith.

"So, you checked for a pulse?" Officer Rosmus asked as she also placed two fingers against Edith's cold, wrinkled neck, checking for a pulse and finding none. The officer then called in the coroner to come as she investigated Edith's untimely death before they removed the body from the house.

By the time the coroner arrived at the scene, Edith's body had become colder and stiffer.

"Do you think she suffered?" Sara asked, hoping that she hadn't. She checked Edith's fingernails for skin, just in case she had scratched her attacker. However, she didn't find any. There were no signs of Edith struggling with her assailant, which may indicate that she hadn't. Edith was weak with fragile bones; it wouldn't take much for anyone of any size to place a pillow over her face and suffocate her to death. But Sara couldn't tell the officer this, because if she did, she would have to reveal everything from before she arrived in this town. She couldn't tell Rosmus about Brad.

"No. I think she passed away quickly in her sleep. In my opinion, it's the best way to go. I believe she didn't suffer, but we'll do a full autopsy and find out the cause of death," Officer Rosmus stated.

"Oh," Sara whispered. She didn't want to think about what they would do to this poor, sweet lady. To her, cutting her open just didn't seem right.

"It's a good thing you're staying here in this house. Who knows how long she would have been lying in here if you weren't living here? She doesn't have a family, you know, and not too many people stop in to visit with her. Well, that I know of," Officer Rosmus said.

Sara nodded at this because she recalled the conversation she had with Edith the morning after arriving here. Edith's husband had passed away many years ago, leaving her alone in the house. They had no children of their own. All Edith had were the people here in Craven Falls. It seemed sad to Sara to live a life so sheltered. Edith must have been lonely in this big house.

"I'll have to call around and see if she had a Will written up and what she wanted done with her remains," Rosmus said.

Sara nodded, and for the first time since she had met Officer Rosmus, she realized that this woman had no emotions whatsoever. She didn't display any—not in her posture or facial expressions. She seemed cold and unlovable, and if anyone were to ask Sara, that's what she would tell people. Officer Rosmus was a cold-hearted person who showed no empathy.

"I can look through her things here and see if I can find anything. I'm sure she has a file somewhere containing what you need," Sara replied.

"Thanks, that will help. Well, we'd better take her to the morgue and get started," Officer Rosmus said as she turned away from Sara and walked out of the bedroom.

Sara nodded again. She wasn't sure what to do now. She didn't have the right to live in this house, did she? But where else could she go? She didn't want to leave, yet she couldn't stay. Could she?

Mick arrived as they were removing Edith's body from

the house and placing it into a van that had the words "Craven Falls Mortuary" written on its side.

"Oh, my God, what happened?" Mick asked.

"I found Edith in her bed this morning," Sara replied. "She passed away in her sleep. They're taking her to the morgue to find out what the cause of death was."

Tears streamed down Mick's face. "Oh, God, I can't imagine what you're going through. Finding Edith in her bed like that." Mick shook her head and looked down at the floor. "I'm so sorry."

Officer Rosmus, still standing in the foyer, nodded at Mick as she entered, then left, following the men out of the house without saying another word.

Mick wiped her eyes as Sara closed the door, locking the deadbolt in place. She knew that if Edith's attacker was out there, he might come back for her if he or she didn't know that Sara was upstairs sleeping the whole time. But just as the thought entered her mind, she recalled the noise outside her bedroom door. Whoever had been here last night stood outside her bedroom door but didn't come in. Why? This, she didn't know.

Sara walked into the kitchen, with Mick following behind her. She had completely forgotten about the coffee she had made and poured herself a cup.

"What's this?" Mick asked as she stood beside the counter, picking up the photo on the counter and turning it over in her hand. "It looks like…" Mick didn't finish her words as Sara came up beside her and snatched the picture from her hand.

Sara swallowed.

"Is that you in the photo?" Mick asked. "Who's the man

with you?"

Sara didn't want to answer any of her questions, not now or ever.

She had torn the picture into pieces the night she had left town and thrown them in the wastebasket. And now she was holding the same picture in her hand. Someone had taped the photo back together with Scotch tape. This meant that Brad was here, and he had been inside this house last night.

Her mind flicked back to last night when she heard the floorboards creak outside her bedroom door. She initially thought it was Steve, but now she realized it had to have been Brad and not Steve. But then why hadn't Brad just come into her room? Why leave a photo of them and not confront her? Why not drag her back to their hometown? Or worse, kill her? Was he playing some kind of game? This she didn't know, but that wasn't what frightened her the most. It was that he was here in Craven Falls. He was hiding somewhere, and she had no idea where or when he would make his next move.

Chapter 28

Sara gasped as the thought of Edith returned to her mind. If Brad had been in this house, could he have killed Edith? Had he placed a pillow over her head and suffocated her in her sleep? Oh God, no! Poor Edith. She wouldn't have been able to fight back; Brad was too strong for her. Being all the way upstairs, Sara wouldn't have heard Edith scream or call for help, would she? The walls in this house were thicker than those in homes built today, although she wasn't sure if that was true. She couldn't allow herself to believe she had heard a noise and simply didn't help poor Edith. She wouldn't be able to live with herself if she had heard something and dismissed it as nothing.

Sara walked over to the kitchen table and slumped down in the chair. It was all too much for her to grasp at that moment. If she hadn't come to this town, to Edith's house, and stayed, then Edith would still be alive. But she had come here, and now Edith was dead.

She needed to think about how to get away from Brad, but she wasn't sure how to do it. She considered leaving her home in the middle of the night to free herself from him, but that hadn't seemed effective. If he were in this town and had been in this house, then he already had the advantage over her, knowing where she was staying and how to get inside.

"Sara, what's wrong?" Mick asked as she sat across from Sara. "You may think I'm clueless, but everyone in this town, even I, know that you came here to get away from something or someone. So, my question is, who is the man in the photo, and why is he after you?"

Sara looked up into Mick's eyes. She couldn't keep her life a secret for much longer. Could she confide in Mick? Yes, she could. She could trust Mick, even if Laura said that she couldn't.

"If I tell you everything, promise me you won't tell anyone? And you know that if he sees you hanging around with me, your life will also be in danger," Sara said as she watched Mick's eyes widen with each word she spoke.

Mick nodded and swallowed. "Okay, I promise not to say a word to anyone. But why would my life be in danger? Who is this guy?"

Sara started from the beginning and explained to Mick how scared she was, stating that the only thing she knew to do was drive as far away from Brad as possible.

"He'll kill me, Mick. He probably still will. If I'm right and he was in this house last night, I think it's possible that he killed Edith. That he was standing outside my bedroom door. The only thing I don't understand is why he just didn't come into my bedroom and kill me too or drag me out of here? Why couldn't he just leave Edith alone and come after me instead?" Sara cried as realization set in. "It's all my fault. I shouldn't have come here."

"Oh, Sara. What can I do to help?"

"Stay as far away from me as you can," Sara wept. "I don't want you to get hurt or, worse, killed!"

"I'm not leaving your side, Sara. So, if he comes after me, then he must kill me too," Mick said.

Sara shook her head. "I can't lose you, too. I already lost Edith. Please, just save yourself," Sara sobbed.

"Then I guess we need to come up with a plan," Mick replied. "And get this asshole before he knows what hit him."

* * *

Both Sara and Mick searched the entire house. They made sure that Brad wasn't hiding anywhere, waiting to jump out and finish the job he had started. What if she were wrong and it hadn't been Brad who killed Edith? Then that wouldn't explain the photo left in the house. It had to be him. There was no question about it.

Sara still couldn't understand why he hadn't come after her when he had the chance. Did he have a different plan for getting rid of her? But she couldn't think about that now. She had to protect herself and Mick.

As Sara walked through the remaining unused bedrooms upstairs, she knew that Steve had left since there weren't any of his belongings in the room. Come to think of it, she didn't recall seeing his car when he arrived, but then again, she hadn't really paid much attention to what he was driving. Still, a part of her wondered what he was even doing here in this town.

Then a thought entered her mind. Could Steve be the one capable of killing Edith? If so, why? Sara had only met the man twice: once when she was heading to the bathroom and a second time at the café. Another thought popped into her mind: was he real? she seemed to ask herself. Had anyone else seen him, too?

Chapter 29

"Okay, I locked the windows and doors, and I also placed a string of cans over the doorknobs so when someone comes in, we'll be able to hear them," Mick said.

"Okay," Sara replied. "Hey, Mick. Do you remember at the café yesterday when I dropped the pot of coffee? Was there a man standing in front of me?"

"I don't recall, but I was coming from the kitchen, so he may have left before I ran out to help you."

Sara nodded. Then she remembered a man named Steve sitting down in a booth, and after that, Sara left for the day. So, wouldn't Mick have waited on him after she left the café?

Sara said, "The man was tall with blond hair and bluish-green eyes. He was sitting in a booth before I left."

Mick replied, "Oh, yeah, I remember him."

Sara's shoulders relaxed. "You do?"

"Yeah. He was super nice, but…"

"But what?"

"After you left, he asked questions about you, but don't worry, I didn't tell him anything."

"What did he ask you?" Sara asked.

"Oh, just where you were from and how long you have lived here. I told him that I didn't feel comfortable sharing information with a stranger," Mick said. "After that, he just drank his coffee and left. He didn't even leave me a tip."

Sara's mind spun in circles. Why would this man she had

met only twice be asking questions about her? Did Brad send him here? This, she didn't know.

With all that had happened since she woke up this morning, Sara was a little skeptical about staying in this huge Victorian house all by herself. She wondered if she should ask Mick to stay with her, but she didn't want her life to be in danger. She wouldn't be able to live with herself if something bad happened to her, like it had with Edith, but she wasn't sure that Brad had been the one who killed her. She could have died on her own.

Mick said, "I'm staying here with you tonight."

Sara smiled. "Really?" It was as if Mick had read her mind.

"Yeah, we can share the same room, but only if you want to."

"Yes, that would be great. It's a king-size bed," Sara agreed. "Besides, I wouldn't want you in another room after what had happened here.

* * *

Several hours later, Sara heard a knock at the front door. She moved the curtains aside to find Officer Rosmus standing on the other side. She rolled her eyes, as if annoyed by her presence. She unlocked the two deadbolts and removed the chain before opening the door.

"Officer Rosmus, what brings you back here?" Sara asked.

"Mind if I come inside?"

Sara minded, but she stepped back, making room for Rosmus to come in. She closed the door behind her, securing the lock even though a police officer stood two feet in front of her. She couldn't take any chances.

"Paranoid much?" Officer Rosmus muttered.

Sara's brows furrowed. Seriously, now she's making wisecracks about my insecurity. For heaven's sake! Edith is dead, and it all could be because of her. Because Sara stayed here in this house. In this town.

She wanted to scream at the woman in front of her. She wanted to tell her to shut her mouth! That she was a heartless bitch! But she didn't and couldn't say these things. Not because the woman was a police officer, but because that wasn't Sara. She didn't get pissed off and yell at people, but maybe she should. Maybe she should let the people around her see how she felt.

"Have you found something?" Sara asked.

"Nothing yet. I just wanted to look around Edith's room," Rosmus replied.

"Is there something I should know about? Did you miss something?" Sara wondered if the officer had realized that someone killed Edith. Murdered her, instead of dying in her sleep.

Chapter 30

Sara followed Officer Rosmus into Edith's bedroom. She stood in the doorway while Rosmus walked around the room, scanning the floor with the beam of a small flashlight in her hand. Sara found it odd to search the room with only a finger-sized flashlight, so she flicked the switch on the wall, flooding the room with more light.

Officer Rosmus looked at Sara with her beady eyes. Had the officer not wanted the light on to assist in searching for whatever she was looking for? Sara thought it would help, but apparently, it had only annoyed the officer. So, Sara flicked the light back off.

Officer Rosmus shot her another look. "What are you doing?" Rosmus shouted, her face reddening. "Quit touching the light switch!"

"Sorry," Sara muttered. "I thought I was helping. It looked too dark in the room. Not sure how you're able to see with only that thing."

"This thing is called a flashlight, and it can spot things you might normally miss using fluorescent light. Besides, how can I concentrate when you keep turning the light on and off? How does that help me find anything? You're making my eyes lose focus!" Officer Rosmus yelled. "Now, all I see are spots."

"Sorry," Sara said and flicked the light back on before she turned and walked away. God, she was just trying to help, and Officer Rosmus bit off her head.

Officer Rosmus left thirty minutes later, not even saying goodbye to Sara. All Sara heard was the click of the deadbolt followed by the door opening and closing. The moment she heard the noise; she hurried to the door and locked it before anyone else could enter. Why was she feeling so fearful, as Officer Rosmus had pointed out? Did she believe Brad would cause a scene? No, he would wait until it was dark before launching the attack. In the past, he had never abused her when other people were present. But this still didn't explain why he hadn't pursued her last night when he had the opportunity.

⁓ ⁓ ⁓

That night, as tired as Sara was, she didn't sleep for more than a few minutes at a time. She kept hearing things that weren't there—or were they there? She tried to convince herself that she was imagining them. Either way, she wasn't getting any sleep tonight. Maybe one of them should have volunteered to stay up?

Sara lay next to Mick, listening to her sleep. Every so often, Mick made a gurgling sound, as if something were lodged in her throat. God, she hoped Mick wouldn't start choking on the phlegm that seemed to block her airway. She couldn't lose another person in this town. Then the police would think she caused their deaths, but she knew she had nothing to do with Abby, Robyn, or Edith.

Her mind swam in circles as she lay there. She should just pack the few things she owned and leave. Mick didn't deserve any of this. She couldn't let anything happen to the one friend she had made in this town. The one person who has stood by her through this whole ordeal. Because if Brad were the one in this house last night who had killed Edith, then she needed to run and get the hell out of here before anyone, including herself, got hurt.

Sara's eyes snapped open at the sound of a noise downstairs. Something had fallen and crashed to the floor.

She sprang into a sitting position, listening.

Silence.

She heard no sound.

Her eyes scanned the room, but it was too dark. The moonlight shining through the window didn't even cast a glimmer of light for her to see inside. Not that she thought anyone was in the bedroom with them. She would have heard them open the door, but she had locked it before going to bed.

She turned to look at Mick, who was sleeping beside her, but he wasn't there. When had Mick left? She hadn't felt him get out of bed. Sara must have fallen asleep, and Mick must have slipped out of bed.

Sara slid out from beneath the blankets and hurried to the bedroom door. It was unlocked, indicating that Mick had left the room. Well, of course, she had. She wasn't in the bedroom with her; she knew that much.

Sara placed her hand on the cold metal knob and turned it. The door squeaked as she opened it. Holding her breath, Sara wondered if doing so would silence the door. She wasn't sure, but she was determined to find Mick before something terrible happened to her, praying that it wasn't too late.

The floorboards creaked beneath her weight as she tiptoed into the hall.

She stopped.

Listened.

Nothing.

She heard no sound.

Sweat bubbled along the hairline at the back of her neck before sliding down under her T-shirt. Suddenly, she felt hot. It was as if she was having a hot flash; had the temperature in the house risen since they went to sleep? She wasn't sure.

Her heart pounded so hard she felt nauseous. She couldn't allow herself to get sick; Mick needed her. Hesitant, she stepped toward the stairs that would lead her to the main floor. A light from the direction of the kitchen caught her eye.

She laughed inside.

Mick was in the kitchen and had dropped something. There was nothing wrong. She felt relieved by this. Her mind had jumped to the conclusion that something was wrong. Mick was fine and was probably getting something to eat. She needed to calm down and not panic.

Sara glided down the stairs, her focus on the still locked *front door. There was nothing to worry about,* she thought.

Once her feet touched the wooden floor below, she felt a cold draft caress her legs, causing the unshaved hair on her legs to stand straight up. The cold air was coming from the kitchen. Was the back door open?

Sara hurried into the room. She saw pieces of glass on the floor. Her eyes scanned the kitchen; it was empty. She didn't see Mick anywhere. Rushing toward the back of the house, she found the back door wide open, yet still no Mick. She grabbed a coat from the hook beside her and stepped outside. The wind blew her hair away from her face, drying the sweat on her back that had formed just minutes before.

She scanned the backyard for Mick but didn't see her.

Should she call her name? What if Brad were out here? Then he would hear her, and it would be all over. But what about Mick? She couldn't leave her out here. She had to find her.

"Mick," Sara whispered. "Mick, are you out here?"

Nothing.

She didn't even hear any animals moving in the woods as she stood on the back porch, staring out at the darkness before her. She only felt the pounding of her heart thumping beneath her chest.

Where was Mick?

Chapter 31

Again, her mind raced. Where was Mick? Oh God, had Brad taken him? She shook her head from side to side as tears sprang from her eyes. She needed to find Mick before he hurt her, hoping she wasn't too late.

She ran back inside and up the stairs. She slipped into a pair of jeans and threw on a sweatshirt. She sprinted back downstairs and into the kitchen. Once the boots were on her feet and she had zipped the coat up to her neck, she grabbed the flashlight from the shelf by the back door and stepped outside. She hurried down the porch steps as if she were on fire and onto the frozen ground below. She pushed the button, and the light from the flashlight flooded all around her.

She moved the light back and forth. Her eyes scanned the wood line, listening and watching. She had to be dreaming this and wished that she would wake the hell up! But there was no way this was a dream. She felt the freezing cold air on her face as it prickled her skin, like water turning to ice. She blinked away the burning chill in her eyes, trying to keep them from drying out. You can't feel things like that when you're asleep. This she was sure of.

First, she ran to the garage and went inside. She looked in her car. It was empty. Well, of course, it was. Did she think Mick would be inside? Well, yes, if she were hiding from someone.

She moved the light around the garage but saw nothing.

There was no sign of anyone having been inside since she was there yesterday. She stepped back through the door, closed it, and stood outside. She wanted to stay in the garage, where the cold, bitter temperatures didn't sting her flesh, but she wouldn't find Mick that way. She had no choice but to go into the woods and look for her.

Up ahead, she saw a path or what seemed to be a trail at one time, worn as if someone had walked it daily. Maybe not recently, not since Sara had arrived in this town. She wished it had snowed so she could see tracks, but that would make things too easy. Nothing in life was easy; this she knew. With the ground solid, there was no way to see any tracks. She wouldn't know if Mick had gone into these woods. She had only assumed that he had because Mick left the back door open. What was the saying? Never assume.

She turned around and saw Edith's house in the distance. If she went too far, would she be able to find her way back? Maybe she should wait and look for Mick in the morning when it was light out. But what if it was too late? All because she was afraid of getting lost in the woods. She wouldn't be able to live with herself if something happened because she chose to wait until daylight. Mick would be dead.

She moved forward, stepping on branches that snapped under her boots. *So much for keeping quiet,* she thought. She waved the flashlight around but didn't see anything. *This was stupid. She would not find her in the dark.* Or was she just too afraid to be out here? Out here, she would be fair game. Brad could snatch her up, and no one would know. Well, of course, they would know. Her car was in the garage. They wouldn't think she'd left this town on foot. Then they would go looking for her, right? Yes, of course. She knew that Officer Rosmus would come looking for her, wouldn't she? Sara wasn't so sure about that. Rosmus wasn't a fan of Sara.

She turned around and headed back toward the house. Once she was close enough to see the Victorian home and its elegant wood trim, which showcased the house's beauty, she felt relieved and safe, but her shoulders were stiff and hard as rock. She wanted to reach under her coat and rub the tightness away, but it would have to wait until she was inside, out of the cold.

She quickened her pace, wanting nothing more than to feel the warmth on her face. She stopped when she reached the edge of Edith's yard and looked up.

She watched as the kitchen light went out.

Chapter 32

She closed her eyes and opened them again, hoping that she had imagined the light flickering off, but she hadn't. The house sat in complete darkness before her. Maybe the power had gone out. Yes, this was possible; she laughed to herself. She nodded in agreement as if she were talking to someone, but there was no one there with her.

Sara looked across the street, but from where she stood, she couldn't see the buildings or houses that lined the road. Edith's house was on a hill. She would have to walk to the front of the house to see if there were lights on inside those homes. But wouldn't there be streetlights? She had to think back to remember if she had seen any streetlights along the road. Her mind drew a blank. She wasn't sure. She had never been outside after dark. She had paid little attention once she was inside the house with Edith. Nor could she recall whether there had been lights beside the road when she arrived.

Then a thought came to her. What if Mick was in the house, and she had turned off the light and gone back to bed? Mick would surely notice that Sara wasn't in bed. That she was missing, wouldn't he? Then he would come looking for her like Sara had gone looking for Mick.

Sara raced across the yard and up the stairs to the back door. She turned the knob, but it was locked.

"Are you kidding me?" she mumbled. Had she accidentally locked the door on her way outside earlier? She wasn't sure, but it was possible. Though a part of her doubted that she had, because she was sure that she hadn't closed the door when she walked out onto the porch. Mick probably saw that the door was unlocked and locked it before heading back upstairs to bed.

Now what was she going to do? She could knock, hoping that Mick would hear her and come downstairs to check out the noise and let her inside. But what if Mick couldn't hear her from all the way upstairs, just as Sara hadn't heard Edith when she was being killed in the room below her? Sara decided that she would first look for a way in before causing a scene and waking the neighbors by pounding on the door for Mick to hear her. They would surely call Officer Rosmus, and she would come out here pissed off, no doubt. Who wouldn't be when it was the middle of the night? Well, Sara had no idea what time it was.

She looked around for a key but didn't find one in the usual hiding places, like under the mat where most people kept a key or under flowerpots. What was she going to do now? It was freezing out here. She couldn't stay outside much longer without risking hypothermia, as the temperatures had dropped into the single digits.

She could try the front door, but she doubted Edith had hidden a key outside. She would have been too afraid of someone coming inside while she was asleep. Plus, there were several deadbolts on the door. Even if she found a key, would it unlock all the locks? Well, she wouldn't know unless she checked. Besides, what did she have to lose? She was already outside in the freaking cold.

She jogged to the front of the house, primarily to stay warm. She checked all the obvious places again but found nothing. With no other option left, she had to either pound on the door or ring the doorbell for Mick to let her in.

Sara did just that. She rang the doorbell repeatedly, but Mick didn't come downstairs. Maybe she was already fast asleep? She knew that some people fell asleep quickly and were dead to the world, but Sara didn't think that was the case. She could feel in her bones that something was very wrong.

She would have to break the window downstairs. She decided to break the one at the back of the house, just in case someone saw her and called the police, thinking she was a burglar. Again, she didn't want Officer Rosmus coming out to the house.

She turned around, hurried down the stairs, almost slipping on the frost-covered steps, and ran to the back of the house. She saw a rock the size of her hand, picked it up, then dropped it. She didn't need the rock; she had a flashlight to use. Standing on the back porch, she tapped on the window with the flashlight. It cracked. Using more force this time, glass shattered onto the floor inside the small mudroom.

She placed the flashlight in her coat pocket, reached inside, and unlocked the latch. A gust of wind pushed against her, causing her to lose her footing. The arm of her coat snagged on a piece of broken glass still attached to the window, ripping her coat. She was thankful that it had not cut her.

She pushed the window up and climbed inside. Once inside, she turned and closed the window behind her, deciding she should cover it given the low temperatures outside.

She went in search of a garbage bag to seal the broken window. When she finished covering it, she shut the doors of the mudroom and kitchen. She shrugged off her coat and boots, placing the flashlight on the kitchen table. She walked to the wall and flicked the switch. No light came on. Had the power gone out after all? Sara moved to the opposite side of the room and peered out the kitchen window. She saw light coming from the house across the street. Fear flooded through her body. She whipped her head around the room, her eyes darting between the stove and the microwave.

Nothing.

No numbers appeared on any of the appliances, and no lights were on anywhere in the house. This indicated that someone had cut the power to the house.

Chapter 33

Suddenly, she felt as though she was suffocating in the large kitchen. She kept her back against the counter while her eyes remained focused on the doorway. She navigated along the counter, slinking toward the block of cutlery knives near the stove. She slid the chef's knife out from its designated slot.

If Brad was in the house, she wasn't going down without a fight. He would have to kill her because she wasn't going back with him. She would not let him make her believe that he hadn't killed that boy in cold blood back in Bristol—the boy who only wanted to be Sara's friend.

Brad felt jealous when he saw Sara with her friends, especially Jay. They had met up at the library after school to study for their Physics test. Brad had made it clear to Sara that she belonged to him and no one else. He warned that if he ever caught her with another guy, he would kill him, and then he would come after her.

The night Sara left her hometown behind was the night she saw Brad beating Jay to death behind the school. It had been dark out, just like tonight. She had received a text that he would pick her up after school. But she texted him back that she was going to the library to study. Brad must have been watching as she and Jay left the library later that evening. Sara told Jay that she would be fine and that he didn't have to worry about her. Jay left, walked around the building, and crossed the field to get home; Brad must have been waiting for him.

She waited on the steps outside the library for Brad, who never showed up. When he didn't arrive, she started her walk home. As she reached the edge of the school, she heard a noise and walked around the library building. She couldn't believe what she saw, but instead of helping Jay, she ran as fast as she could all the way home. That was when she found herself in Craven Falls, knowing that Brad would come for her next.

She gripped the knife tightly in her right hand. Her eyes moved around the room as they adjusted to the darkness. She spotted the kitchen table and chairs across the room, then the large center island in the middle. Her gaze settled on the doorway that would lead her to the rest of the house—one engulfed in complete darkness, with many shadowy corners for someone to hide. She knew she couldn't remain in the kitchen. She needed to confront Brad one last time and put an end to this. He wouldn't kill her as well. He wasn't going to beat her the way he had beaten and killed her friend Jay. A thought crossed her mind. Had he killed others? God, she hoped not.

She inched her way down the counter along the sink and passed the coffeemaker. The foyer came into view, and beyond that, she could just see the outline of the sofa in the living room. She swallowed and stepped through the doorway until she reached the foot of the stairs. She looked up but saw nothing. However, that didn't mean Brad wasn't up there or whoever was in the house. She decided to check the remaining rooms on the first floor before going upstairs.

She crept down the hall and stood in front of Edith's bedroom. She pushed the door inward, the hinges moaning as it opened. The room was pitch black. She couldn't see anything, not even the bed. That was when she realized that the blinds were closed. But who had closed them? Her mind flicked back to earlier like a movie projector clicking on each scene. Officer Rosmus was the last person in this room, wasn't she? Or had Mick come in here and closed the curtains? One of them had. This she was sure of because she hadn't.

Without thinking, Sara reached her hand along the wall and flicked the switch. No light filled the room. She had forgotten all about the power being out because she was frightened of what or who was in this house.

Disappointment settled in the pit of her stomach as she remembered that she had left the flashlight on the kitchen table. She needed to go back for it. Although the thought of walking through the darkened rooms terrified her, she had no other choice. She had to return for the flashlight.

She felt her way back toward the kitchen and to the table where she had left the flashlight, but it wasn't there. Yes, she was sure she had placed it on the table before taking off her coat. Or maybe she had thought about doing it, and her mind had wandered, leading her to forget? Yes, this was exactly what had happened; she was sure of it.

She turned and felt the pockets of her coat. Nope, no flashlight in either pocket. So, where had it gone? She was sure that she had seen no one in the kitchen with her. But that didn't mean there wasn't someone somewhere else in the house.

The floorboards creaked in the next room. She threw herself against the wall and closed her eyes, waiting for whoever was on the other side to appear and bring it all to an end. Brad would finally kill her, and she wouldn't have to hide from him again. Except that no one came. No one walked through the doorway into the kitchen. Had she imagined the noise? Maybe it had come from upstairs instead of the other room. Yes, this was a possibility.

She held her breath, listening to the sounds in the house. That's when she realized it was the wind that had caused the creaking sound. The house was old. In that moment, she heard a gust of wind howling outside, then the boards that held the house together moaned and creaked. Then, there was nothing but silence.

She exhaled and let her shoulders relax. She was being a scaredy-cat, although she had every right to be. Exhaustion washed over her, and her body drooped. She became extremely tired, as if she were drugged, and needed to get to bed before she collapsed right here on the floor. She walked out of the kitchen and stood at the bottom of the stairs. A faint smell lingered in the air, making her stomach clench and her head feel fuzzy. It was a smell she couldn't distinguish.

She grabbed the handrail and started up the stairs. So much had happened tonight, yet she acted as if all was right in the world. She didn't feel afraid of anything or anyone. She wasn't sure what had come over her. Had she completely given up and decided that if Brad wanted to kill her, then so be it? She didn't know what was wrong with her. She felt dizzy and needed to lie down.

She strolled to the bedroom that she and Mick were sharing and opened the door. Thankfully, Mick hadn't locked it when she went back to bed. Sara noticed a mound beneath the blankets on the other side of the bed. Her body grew sluggish, and she sauntered over to the bed. She placed the knife on the nightstand next to her and crawled beneath the cold blankets.

She wasn't sure what had come over her. She felt lethargic. Was it from the day's events? From the lack of sleep her body had fought off earlier and had finally caught up to her? All she knew was that she didn't want to think anymore. All she wanted was to sleep.

She felt extremely dizzy.

Feeling very tired.

She closed her eyes and fell into a deep sleep.

Chapter 34

When Sara woke the following morning, she felt rested but also tingly all over. She couldn't remember taking anything—just smelling an odor before coming upstairs to bed.

She closed her eyes, allowing the events from the day before to unfold in her mind. Everything that had happened started with Edith. A tear escaped and fell onto the pillow. Why, of all people, had Edith been the one to die? Not that she would have wanted someone else to die in Edith's place because she wouldn't wish that upon anyone. Why did anyone have to die at all?

First, her friend Jay and now Edith. She was afraid for Mick. Sara needed to get Mick away from her before Brad killed him too. She wished she could go back in time and had never met Brad, never even dated him.

She flipped onto her back and stared at the ceiling before turning her head to face Mick beside her. The blankets covered Mick's head as if she were cold or didn't like the light shining through the curtains. She couldn't see Mick's face because she was turned away, facing the wall.

Sara reached over and was about to nudge her friend's shoulder but thought better of it. Mick was probably just as exhausted as Sara had been, and she would let her sleep a little longer.

She slid out of bed, padded to the door, and opened it. "What the hell!" Sara screamed when she saw Officer

Rosmus standing outside in the hall. "What are you doing? You scared the living shit out of me!" Sara thought she could see a hint of a smirk forming on the officer's lips. *Did she think that it was funny to scare me like that*? Sara wondered.

"I'm sorry, I didn't mean to frighten you. I was just about to check the room. I wasn't sure if you had stayed here or left town," Officer Rosmus said.

"Well, I don't really have anywhere else to stay," Sara replied, although she wasn't sure how much to tell the officer. She knew that she would leave today because she was sure that Brad was here in town and was coming to get her.

"I'm glad that you are still here. I'll need you *not* to leave town until we have finished the investigation," Officer Rosmus stated.

Investigation? Sara thought. "When did this turn into an investigation? I thought Edith died of natural causes?"

"As did I, but we have found some evidence that proves otherwise."

"Oh, no," Sara gasped.

"Is there anyone else in the house with you? Is Mick here? I had a call come into the station that she never came home last night," Officer Rosmus questioned as she shifted the subject.

Sara nodded. "Yes, she's still sleeping." Sara tilted her head toward the bed behind her.

"Mind if I talk to her? Her aunt is pretty worried about her."

"Aunt?" Sara asked. She could have sworn that Mick had said parents last night, or? Sara became confused. Had Mick even mentioned asking her parents? No, she had specifically said that she would stay here, not that she had to ask if she could spend the night. In fact, they had never really had a conversation about Mick's living arrangements. Though Sara had questioned why Mick always walked to Edith's instead of having Sara pick her up at her home. She'd have to ask her later. She just hoped that Mick trusted her enough to confide in her, just as Sara had about Brad.

"Yes, her Aunt Mabel. She's lived with her since she was a child. Her parents died in a plane crash. Sad really, but Mabel has been good to Mick," Rosmus said, bowing her head as if in prayer.

Was she about to cry? Sara wondered.

"So, do you mind if I talk to her? I must get back to the station and follow up on some evidence we found."

"Evidence? Does it have to do with Edith?"

"Well, just between you and me," Officer Rosmus leaned in as if she were telling Sara a secret. "It's none of your business!"

Sara stepped back as if she had been slapped across the face. She couldn't understand why this woman was so hostile towards her. Sara had done nothing wrong. Besides, there had been deaths in this town long before she arrived. They didn't occur when she drove into town. So, what the hell was this woman's problem with her?

Officer Rosmus pushed past Sara and entered the room. "Mick, are you up? I need to talk to you." There was no reply. Rosmus reached out her hand and nudged Mick's shoulder.

Still nothing.

Rosmus peeled back the blanket.

Chapter 35

"What the…?" Officer Rosmus shouted as she stepped away from the bed, pressing her back against the wall behind her.

Sara ran over to see what was wrong with Mick, when she saw Steve lying in the same bed she had slept in last night. His face was covered in blood. Beaten with a blunt object, maybe a hammer with claw-like edges, as there were deep cuts all along his face.

One of his eyes bulged out of its socket, and the other was completely absent. Gone as if the eye had never existed. Just a hollow, bloody shell. The rest of his face had chunks missing, and there was a large hole in the side of his head above his right ear, which Sara was more than sure caused his death.

Sara absorbed the gruesome scene, placing a hand on her stomach and covering her mouth with the other. She bolted from the room toward the bathroom and violently heaved into the toilet as images of Steve flashed in her mind. When she finished, she sat back on her heels and shook her head as if that would dislodge the thoughts, but she knew she would never forget, just like Edith. She had just met the man two days ago, and now he was dead. She was sure Brad had killed him.

"No, no, no," Sara muttered. It was all her fault. Brad must have seen them at the café and thought that something was going on between the two of them. But, as usual, nothing had happened. Just as if nothing had happened between her and Jay. When was he going to stop?

"Where's Mick?" Officer Rosmus asked from the bathroom doorway.

Sara shook her head. "I don't know. Last night, I went downstairs and saw that the back door was open. I went looking for her outside but couldn't find her. When I got back to the house, the light went off in the kitchen, and I assumed that Mick hadn't come outside at all. So, I came back inside and went back to bed. I saw a mound of blankets beside me and had thought she was sleeping," Sara sobbed. Tears and snot slithered into her open mouth. "My head felt fuzzy last night, and I was just too tired to wake her."

"So, you had no idea that this man was in bed with you, and someone had beaten him to death?"

"No!" Sara shouted. "What kind of person do you think I am? I didn't kill him. I didn't kill Edith either."

"I never said you did, unless you're confessing to the crime."

"For fuck's sake! **I. Didn't. Kill. Them!**" Sara yelled as she stood facing Officer Rosmus. "What is your problem with me? Ever since I met you, you have been blaming me for the things that have happened in this town. When clearly, Craven Falls had murders here way before I ever arrived!"

Officer Rosmus stepped back into the hall, away from Sara. "Well," Rosmus began. "It's not that I think you had anything to do with the recent deaths. It's just that it's a coincidence that four people—make that five, because Mickey is missing—have been found alive or dead in your presence."

"Well, I didn't kill them. I only met that man." Sara

pointed toward the bedroom where Steve was lying. "Twice. In fact, we hadn't said more than a few words to one another."

"What did you two talk about?" Officer Rosmus asked.

Sara's shoulders sank. She felt exhausted by the conversation they were having, which seemed to lead nowhere but in circles.

The first time we met, I accidentally ran into him right there outside my bedroom door.

"Did he say anything to you?"

"Well, after I apologized for running into him, he said that there was nothing to be sorry for. Then I went into the bathroom and got ready for school," Sara explained.

"And the second time?" Officer Rosmus asked.

"Was at the café. I had dropped the coffeepot. He asked if I was okay, and that was the last time I had seen him. In fact, you were there when it happened. Sitting at the counter with some guy by the name of Reece."

Officer Rosmus nodded. "I will call this in, but don't plan on going anywhere. You'll need to stay here in town. I'll set you up at my sister's house later today until we get things situated. Do you have a problem with that?"

"No, but what about Mick? Since it's clear she wasn't the one in the house last night, then where did she go?" Sara asked.

"I don't know, but I'll have a couple of people here in town look for her. You said you thought she might have gone into the woods last night?"

Sara nodded.

"Okay, well, then we'll start there," Officer Rosmus stated.

"I need to get my things from the room," Sara said as she squeezed through the doorway of the bathroom and headed into the bedroom where Steve was lying. She was sure that it had been Brad who had done this. Which told her that he was definitely here in town, and he wasn't leaving without her. That he was planning some kind of reunion, and she needed to be ready.

Sara saw Officer Rosmus standing in the doorway, watching her as she quickly gathered her belongings from the drawer and placed them into her duffle bag. She was moving fast because she didn't want to remain in this room any longer than necessary.

\+ + +

Sara sat at the kitchen table, nursing a cup of coffee downstairs while the policemen gathered Steve's body to take him to the same place where Edith was: the morgue.

It hadn't hit her until this very moment as she tried to put the events of this morning into perspective. How had Officer Rosmus gotten into the house this morning? The front and back doors were both locked. Sara hadn't checked the window but doubted that the officer would have climbed through it. So, how did she get in? Did she have a key? Sara didn't think so. It all just seemed strange to her that Rosmus showed up the way she did. And the look on her face when she opened the bedroom door. Rosmus looked surprised to see her, at least for a second, before smirking. Something was up, and Sara would have to be more careful around Officer Rosmus. She didn't trust her one bit.

Not only did she have to worry about Brad, but also about Officer Rosmus. There was something about her that

Sara couldn't grasp, like an itch you couldn't scratch. Sara's back stiffened when she heard Mick's name mentioned in the next room.

"Okay, once we're finished removing the body, I want you to search for Mick. Start from behind the house and work your way through the woods. If you find anything, call it in at once," Officer Rosmus said.

"Where will you be?" a male voice asked.

"At the morgue, looking for evidence. I will find out who is doing this," Officer Rosmus replied.

Sara stood up and hurried to where her coat hung, slipping it on. She slid her feet into her boots and quietly opened the mudroom door. Then, she exited through the back door and descended the stairs toward the woods. If Officer Rosmus wasn't in a hurry to search for Mick, she would look for him instead of sitting around.

She wanted to.

No, she needed to find Mick and prayed that Brad hadn't gotten to her first.

Chapter 36

It was now late morning, almost noon, when Sara headed into the woods to look for Mick. She scanned the forest floor for clues to see if someone had been out there, but found nothing—not one footprint or shoeprint. She wouldn't find any; the ground was solid, frozen from the low temperatures. The only shoeprints she saw, she believed, were hers from last night, but she couldn't be positive. They may have been there before she ever arrived in Craven Falls.

She remained on the path she had seen the night before and followed it away from Edith's house. She turned and glanced over her shoulder twice to check if anyone was following or watching her. She didn't see anyone.

She came upon a fork in the path, unsure of which way to go. She studied both options and chose the one on the right, which led her deeper into the woods. Was she being foolish for coming out here alone? Yes, probably, but she needed to put a stop to this. She had to make Brad stop killing the people who mattered to her.

Sara wrapped her arms around herself as the cold air chilled her body. She was freezing and pulled the hood up over her head so only a small portion of her face remained visible. She wished she had gloves and remembered them sitting on the bench in the mudroom after leaving the house. Well, she wasn't going back for them now. She shoved her hands into the pockets of her coat and continued through the woods.

The farther she walked, the more the woods appeared the same to her. She hadn't encountered anything—no tracks or buildings, not even a shack used by hunters.

Sara looked up at the sky. The sun was at high noon, which meant that she hadn't been gone long. Maybe she should turn around and head back in the same direction she had come. She would follow the path to avoid getting lost, but she didn't want to stop looking for Mick. Although she had reasons to believe that if she hadn't come across her yet, then she wouldn't find her.

She stopped and scanned the woods around her. There was nothing out here; she was sure of that. So why had she come here in the first place? Well, she knew why, but now she felt foolish for doing it.

She turned around to head back to Edith's when she noticed a movement to her left. She stood still, waiting and listening for anything that would confirm whether what she thought she saw was real. She believed it could be an animal rather than a person.

She placed one foot in front of the other and left the trail behind. She tried to be careful not to step on any branches, as the noise would give her away if someone were hiding. She walked a little further, then paused and listened. Sara wasn't sure, but she could have sworn she heard a moan.

She continued until she spotted an arm hanging over a log. She rushed over to the log and saw Mick on the other side.

"Oh, God! Mick, are you okay?" Sara shouted.

A shallow moan came from Mick, prompting Sara to drop to the ground beside him. She rolled Mick onto his back. Although she wasn't bleeding, Sara knew that something was very wrong because Mick wasn't responding to her presence.

"Mick, open your eyes?" Sara pleaded as she gently padded Mick's cheek.

Mick opened her eyes, which seemed to sparkle at Sara as if smiling at her. "Sara," Mick croaked, then her eyes closed.

Chapter 37

Sara could see Edith's house in the distance. She had made several stops along the way to catch her breath, but she continued walking with Mick in her arms. She was still alive, though her pulse was weak. Sara had to get Mick help; she couldn't let her die, too.

Sara looked up just as the back door of the house opened and Officer Rosmus stepped out, as if she had known that Sara was outside and needed help.

Sara stopped and fell to her knees, laying Mick down on the ground. It seemed to take only seconds before Officer Rosmus stood above her, breathing harder than Sara, despite her having carried Mick through the woods.

"Is she?" Officer Rosmus asked. "Dead?"

"Not yet," Sara replied. "We should get her into the house and get her warm. I think she has hypothermia."

Officer Rosmus scooped Mick into her arms as if she weighed nothing at all. The officer hurried toward the house and climbed the stairs. Rosmus kicked the bottom of the door, and it swung inward. She slipped through the opening and placed Mick on the sofa in the living room.

Sara grabbed as many blankets as she could find and placed them on top of Mick.

"We should rub her legs and arms to get the blood flowing. It may help warm her faster," Officer Rosmus suggested.

Sara began to move her arms vigorously up and down Mick's legs.

"I'll call for an ambulance," Rosmus said.

* * *

Sara paced the lobby, waiting to hear from the nurse or doctor caring for Mick. She looked up at the clock on the wall; it was just past five in the evening. She couldn't believe how quickly time had flown by. She couldn't recall when she had arrived at the hospital. All she cared about was saving Mick.

"Excuse me?" a woman's voice asked. "Are you Sara? Mickey's friend?"

Sara turned toward the voice, hoping to see a nurse or doctor speaking to her, but instead, she saw a middle-aged woman with cropped jet-black hair. The woman's face was oval-shaped, and her eyes were hazel. She stood with a closed-off demeanor, showing no emotion. Sara didn't recognize her; she hadn't seen her before. Therefore, she shouldn't assume anything about her.

"Yes, I'm Sara," she replied.

The middle-aged woman stepped closer to Sara. "Hi, I'm Mickey's aunt. My name is…"

"Mabel," Sara interrupted.

The woman nodded.

Sara walked the rest of the way and stood in front of Mabel. "Have you heard any news on Mick?" she asked.

"No, not yet. How long do you think she was out there in the freezing cold?" Mabel asked.

Sara shrugged her shoulders but then said, "I think since last night sometime. Maybe one or two in the morning."

"Oh, my God," Mabel whispered, shaking her head. "Thank you so much for finding her. I heard that you were the one who went out into the woods to look for her and had carried her back to the house."

Sara nodded.

"Can we sit?" Mabel asked, flexing her arm toward the chairs to her right.

Sara nodded and turned to the chairs beside them. They sat down and chatted until a man in a white coat entered the room.

"I'm looking for Mickey Thurman's family," the male doctor said.

"Yes," Mabel jumped up from her chair. "I'm Mickey's aunt."

The doctor approached Mabel. "We were able to get her temperature back up to normal. The nurses and I didn't find any damage to her skin or any broken bones. There was no frostbite, which is a good thing, since she wasn't wearing any shoes or socks, not even a coat?" the doctor seemed to question. "I have to say that I'm shocked by this because the temperatures were below normal last night. But it looks like you found her in time."

Mabel turned and glanced at Sara. She smiled and mouthed the words, "*thank you*," then turned back to face the doctor. "When can I see her?" Mabel asked.

"Now, if you'd like. She still needs rest and more fluids, so I want to keep her overnight just to be safe," the doctor said.

Mabel nodded in agreement. "Yes, of course."

"Follow me and I'll take you to her room," the doctor said and turned, walking toward the elevators. "We moved her to a room upstairs on the third floor."

Mabel followed the doctor, then stopped and peered over her shoulder at Sara. "Aren't you coming?" Mabel asked Sara. "I know that Mick will want to see you."

Sara smiled. "Are you sure?"

"Yes."

Sara grabbed her belongings from the chair and hurried to follow Mabel and the doctor. A few minutes later, Sara and Mabel stood beside Mick's bed. Mick opened her eyes and glanced at Mabel and then at Sara.

"Hey, how are you feeling?" Sara asked.

Mick licked her dry and cracked lips. "I'm better now," Mick replied, her voice hoarse.

"Do you want some water?" Mabel asked.

Mick nodded, keeping her gaze fixed on Sara.

Sara wasn't sure what Mick was thinking at that moment, but she could tell something was bothering her. Was Mick glad that she had been the one to find her, or was he disappointed? It was hard to tell. Maybe Mick didn't want to say anything in front of her aunt, but why? What was it that Mick didn't want her aunt to know about?

Mabel handed Sara the cup of water. "I think I'll go get some coffee and let the two of you talk for a bit," Mabel said.

Sara noticed Mick's gaze toward her aunt and almost felt sympathy for Mabel. All Mabel wanted was to ensure Mick was okay, yet Mick pushed her aunt away as if she were some horrible disease.

Sara waited until the door closed before speaking. "Well, that was rude of you. I know I don't know the whole story between the two of you, but she cares about you, Mick. She's devastated about what happened to you. I think she feels responsible."

"Well, she shouldn't!" Mick barked.

Sara thought Mick was about to say more, but she didn't, so she spoke instead. "Are you sure you're, okay? You seem like there's something wrong? Something you're not telling me," Sara asked.

Mick closed her eyes. "He was there last night," Mick whispered as if someone were in the room with them, not wanting them to hear.

"Who? Brad?"

Mick nodded. "I think it was him. I went downstairs to get something to drink, and I saw something or someone standing in the shadows in the living room. I got scared and ran out of the house. I'm so sorry I left you there," Mick said.

"Did you see him? Did he show his face to you?"

Mick shook her head. "I just know it was him. Why?"

Sara swallowed, and then her body shivered as if a coldness had fallen over her. She had to tell Mick who they had found in her bed that morning, which still made her feel nauseous to think about. There was no other way around it. If Sara didn't tell him, she knew that Officer Rosmus would.

Sara told Mick that she looked for her outside and then saw the light flickering off in the kitchen. She had assumed it was her inside the house, and that Mick hadn't gone outside after all. Then Sara mentioned this morning when Officer Rosmus showed up at the house and found Steve's body in the bed they had both slept in last night.

"Oh, my God!" Mick bellowed. "You think that it may have been Steve that I saw and not Brad? But Brad would have been in the house too and would have killed him? Because neither you nor I had done it."

"Yes, it's very possible that Brad killed Steve, for whatever reason." *Not that he had to have a reason,* Sara thought. She knew now that Brad didn't care and would hurt anyone to get to her. But what she didn't understand was why he played this cat-and-mouse game with her. Why didn't he just come after her and get it over with? Why kill the people around her?

Chapter 38

Two hours later, Sara sat at the kitchen table in the house where Officer Rosmus had placed her.

"My sister moved out and hasn't gotten around to selling the house, so you can stay here until things get sorted out," Officer Rosmus said. "I put clean sheets on the bed in the guest room. Not that they had many guests staying here, if any."

"They?" Sara asked.

"My sister Delaney and her daughter, Megan, moved away a couple of weeks ago."

The name Megan rang a bell. The girl from school. Oh, what was her name? Alice, no, Aubrey. Yes, of course. Aubrey had said that Megan left town and that she wasn't aware Megan had a sister named Robyn. A twin sister, in fact, which could be why no one knew the difference between the two girls *if* they had switched places. But why would they do that?

Sara wondered if she should ask Officer Rosmus, who was sitting across from her, these questions. Would she even tell her the truth? There had been a lot of deaths in this town since September—deaths that had nothing to do with Sara herself. She also knew that the recent deaths had no relation to what happened here in the fall. That's why Officer Rosmus was questioning her. Rosmus knew there was a connection somewhere between Sara, Edith's death, and now this man, Steve. It was just a matter of time before the officer figured everything out and understood what had brought Sara to this town.

"I will have an officer patrolling the streets. Here's my direct number if you need me," Officer Rosmus said, pushing her business card across the table.

"I don't have a cell phone," Sara lied. She couldn't tell her about the one in her glove compartment, the one she was afraid to turn on. But what difference did it make now if he, Brad, was already here? Somehow, he had found her. Was Steve the one who had led Brad to her? Or was that all coincidental? She didn't know, but they had to be connected. This she was sure of.

Officer Rosmus looked at her as if she were from another planet, and Sara understood why. What teenager didn't have a cell phone?

"Give me a minute," Rosmus said, as she stood and walked outside. She returned, handing Sara a cell phone. "Here, use this for now. We always carry a few extras in case we lose ours," Rosmus said.

Sara found that strange but nodded and thanked the officer. She knew that it was baloney. She had friends back home whose parents were police officers, and she knew that they didn't keep spare phones around.

"I'll let you get some sleep. There's food in the fridge if you're hungry. I'll be here in the morning to check on you."

"Okay, thank you for everything."

"Yes, well, I just want to find out what's going on here lately and put a stop to it," Rosmus said. "This town has been in chaos for months now. I thought for sure things would be over with when we found out who killed the girl at the high school, but then…" Officer Rosmus stopped talking as if she were about to say something she shouldn't. She cleared her throat, turned away from Sara, and walked out the door without finishing what she was about to say.

Sara sat in the kitchen, staring at the closed door in front of her as she let the officer's words sink in. Was she going to say something about Megan and Robyn? She didn't know, but her curiosity was piqued. She wanted to speak to Aubrey again and to Abby, who was Megan's best friend. Abby would have known if there was something different about her best friend Megan, and if someone was pretending to be her friend, wouldn't she? Yet, Megan and Robyn had nothing to do with what was going on in this town right now. She was sure that Rosmus was hiding something. Still, she would talk to Abby anyway and uncover the underlying cause of what the hell was happening in this town.

Sara needed to distract herself. It was the only way to stop thinking about Brad and that he was in town. It was the only thing she could do to avoid worrying about him coming after her next.

***

In her dream, Sara stood above the body in the road—the same body she had seen and discovered the night she arrived in Craven Falls. It was the night she wished she hadn't driven down the road that led her to this mysterious place she had never heard of before.

But in the dream, she did something different from what she had done the night she arrived. As she stood above the body, she focused on its position, unlike her previous thoughts about how it reminded her of how she slept with one leg bent.

No, this time she focused more on the leg, stretched out and turned in the opposite direction. She held onto that image and allowed her mind to revisit the day when she had stood at the door of the Tanner house, where she found Abby. There was no way she could have walked away without being in excruciating pain. She had a broken bone. Abby had only a cut on her leg. Though badly infected, there was no sign of a fractured bone. Then Sara knelt to the ground to get a better look at the girl's body. She reached out a hand to remove the hood covering the girl's face when she was jerked from her dream.

Bang. Bang. Bang.

Someone was banging on the bedroom door. She sprang out of bed and got to her feet. She placed a hand on her head, feeling dizzy all of a sudden. She had stood up too fast. Then her body fell forward as she tripped over something on the floor. "You stupid idiot," she muttered under her breath, as she looked down to find her clothes lying on the floor beside the bed.

She instinctively extended her arms in front of her and grasped the edge of the wooden dresser to prevent herself from falling to the floor and inflicting more pain. Just before she could reach the door, it swung open, narrowly missing her face as Officer Rosmus rushed in.

"I thought something had happened to you," Officer Rosmus shouted.

Sara regained her footing. She brushed the hair that had fallen into her face away as she stood up.

"I'm fine," she said, though she didn't feel fine. She was about to see the girl's face under the hood, even though she knew it was Abby's, but now she was questioning herself.

Why would she be dreaming about it if she already knew who it belonged to? She remembered talking about the subconscious mind in school. The brain held knowledge that you, as a person, didn't want to face—things you didn't want to recall until it was time, aspects of ourselves we aren't fully aware of.

Sara shook the thoughts from her head and stepped back from the officer until she felt the bed behind her legs and sat down. The mattress sank.

Sara looked up and saw the concern in the officer's face. Perhaps she had been wrong about this woman, and that she did care. She didn't know because the truth was Officer Rosmus didn't seem like the caring type; she knew what one looked like because her grandmother was very loving.

Sara's heart was beating normally again, and she no longer felt the pulse in her ears. "Is there something wrong?" Sara asked.

"No, I just thought… Well, you didn't answer the door when I tried knocking the first time, so I knocked louder. You didn't answer again. You didn't call out that you heard me, so I…" Officer Rosmus paused as if looking for her next set of words, but she didn't say another word. She didn't speak.

"Assumed that I was dead?"

Officer Rosmus nodded.

"Well, I'm not," Sara replied. Though there was so much more she wanted to say to this woman of the law, she held back. It was best that she kept her mouth closed, at least for now.

Chapter 39

Officer Rosmus didn't stay long after the abrupt intrusion of Sara's morning. Once the officer left, Sara showered and changed, and now rummaged through the refrigerator for something to eat. Nothing seemed appealing, so she grabbed a banana hanging from a metal hook on the counter.

As Sara peeled the fruit, she scanned the kitchen—something she hadn't done the night before. If Rosmus' sister Delaney had left, moved out as she had said, then why was the place still furnished? Had she missed that part of the conversation? Maybe it was with all that had happened? She tuned out when Officer Rosmus was talking about the furniture. Why wouldn't you take the furniture and your belongings with you? This seemed a little odd to Sara. Was Delaney planning on buying all new furniture? Well, she didn't know, and did it even matter? No, not really; it just seemed strange, was all. To an outsider like Sara, someone who had arrived here and didn't know the whole story behind the things that had happened here months ago, this would seem abnormal, weird, and maybe bizarre, but this town was uniquely strange.

She tossed the banana peel into the garbage and walked down the hall. She decided to explore what the rest of the house had to offer. She paused in front of the first door she encountered and opened it. The room was fully furnished, just like the rest of the house.

There was a queen-size bed with a gray comforter and decorative pillows on it. On the walls, she saw several pictures. There were two girls; one she knew, Abby. She assumed the other must be Megan, her best friend. She could see the resemblance between Robyn and Megan. They were exactly alike—identical twins, no doubt. It would have been easy to mistake them if they weren't side by side.

She gazed around the room and saw that there were still books on the bookshelves. Sara walked further into the room and began to open the drawers, still filled with clothes. Girls' clothes that she was sure were Megan's too. Again, she found it strange that the owners would have left all this behind. Something wasn't right, and now Sara was curious to know what had happened to Delaney and Megan. There was something wrong with this picture, and she felt that she needed to uncover the truth, even if it didn't concern her. Which it didn't.

Sara searched through the remaining drawers of the dresser, only to confirm what she already knew: more clothes. She walked to the nightstand beside the bed and opened the top drawer. As she rummaged around, she noticed something hiding under what appeared to be a blue scarf. She moved the fabric aside and spotted a journal. Feeling guilty for wanting to read it, she shrugged the guilt away and grabbed the book. She knew that if it was important, Megan would have taken the diary with her. Placing it under her arm, she moved around the room and stopped in front of a desk where she saw a jewelry box.

Sara reached out her hand and opened the lid of the jewelry box. She saw stud earrings and a few hoop earrings—nothing out of the ordinary. She closed the lid and moved to one of the four small drawers. She opened the first drawer, which held more earrings, and moved on to the next until she opened the last drawer and saw something familiar.

Sara grabbed the silver chain, pulling it out of the box. She held it in front of her face. It was the half of the necklace with the letters **ST** and **END** on it. Megan hadn't taken it with her. So, whose necklace was the one that Sara had hanging in her car? She didn't know. But the question remained as to why Megan had taken none of her things with her.

"What the hell do you think you're doing?" said a voice.

Sara cupped the necklace in her palm and spun around to find Officer Rosmus standing in the doorway. Her face was flushed with fury.

"I asked you what you are doing in here?"

"Nothing. I just… I'm sorry," Sara replied, her words scattered. "I didn't mean to snoop." Sara leaned back and closed the small drawer with her hand so Rosmus wouldn't know she was snooping.

"Clearly you did. Get out of this room!" Officer Rosmus shouted. "You are not to be in here! I knew I should have locked the door."

Sara raced past the officer and out of the room. She entered the kitchen, pocketing the necklace in her jeans. Closing her eyes, she took a deep breath, praying that Rosmus didn't see the book hidden under her arm.

Sara slipped the book into the front of her jeans, pulling her shirt over the top. She heard the door to the bedroom slam shut and Rosmus turning the knob to confirm that it was now locked. Sara looked down to ensure the book wasn't visible, tightening the sweater she wore around her waist before turning back to face the irate officer.

"Again, I'm sorry. I didn't mean to meddle. I was just curious," Sara said, leaving out that she wondered why the room still had the girl's things inside. The entire house did. She wanted to ask, but she knew better. Officer Rosmus, she was sure, would lock her in a cell if Sara continued to be a pest.

They looked at one another before Rosmus turned and walked out the front door, leaving Sara alone in the kitchen. She rolled her shoulders back, releasing the tension that had built up in them. Officer Rosmus had to stop appearing unexpectedly. Sara wasn't sure that she could handle any more surprises, though she should be thankful that she was young and her heart was in good health.

Sara walked to the bedroom where she was staying, closed the door behind her, and locked it. Just in case Rosmus returned and barged in like she had this morning.

She pulled the necklace out of her front pocket and examined it. The clasp was broken, which explained why it was in the jewelry box and why Megan wasn't wearing it. She unzipped the front pocket of her overnight bag and placed the necklace inside.

She then climbed onto the bed and sat cross-legged in the center of the mattress. She held the journal she had found in the drawer in Megan's bedroom. She opened the book and began reading.

Halfway through the book, Megan had written about her sister named Robyn and how they would confront their mother. Megan asked herself questions in the journal, pondering why her mother would keep her twin sister a secret from her. Sara read several more pages of the diary until she found a page that discussed her aunt, Officer Rosmus, and that she had…; Sara turned the page, but there was nothing written. Someone had ripped the page out. But why go through all that trouble when they could have just gotten rid of the entire book? Or had Megan changed her mind and, instead of erasing what she wrote, torn the page out? And hidden the journal under a scarf in the drawer?

Sara's brain went into overdrive. She needed to know what had happened to Megan and Delaney, but how was she going to find out? Then she recalled the name Reece written in the book. Now all she had to do was locate him, and she would get the answers she needed.

Chapter 40

Sara sat in her parked car outside Abby's house. If anyone would know something, it would be her. She had been Megan's best friend and had lived in Craven Falls since, well, Sara wasn't sure how long Abby had lived in this town. But she was about to find out.

Sara opened the car door and climbed out. She walked around the front of the car and up the walkway to the front door of Abby's house. She took a deep breath and exhaled before knocking on the door. A few seconds later, the door creaked open. Abby stood in the doorway just as she had the day Sara had found her at the Tanner house.

"Hey, how are you feeling?" Sara asked.

Abby smiled and opened the door, inviting Sara inside to escape the cold.

Sara stood waiting for Abby to say something, but she didn't. Sara was never one to keep quiet; she hated silence. Thus, she would have to do the talking if she wanted answers, considering that was why she was here.

"So… how is the leg?"

"It's better now. Thank you again for helping me," Abby replied.

Sara nodded. She needed to come right out and ask her the questions she had. "Do you mind if we sit? I have a few questions on my mind that I need to ask. That's if you're willing to answer them for me," Sara said, feeling like a reporter.

Abby nodded and led the way to the family room. She sat in the chair by the window and placed her leg on the ottoman. Sara took a seat diagonally so that she could face Abby.

"What is it that you want to know?" Abby asked.

"How long were you and Megan friends?"

"Since we were five."

"Do you know where she may have moved to?"

Abby shook her head. "She was gone before I came back home. You know, when you found me. I haven't spoken to Crystal."

Sara's eyebrows furrowed in confusion.

"Officer Rosmus is Crystal, Megan's aunt," Abby added.

Sara nodded, realizing her mistake. She had known this when she found Robyn's body. Mick had told her. She just had forgotten. Lately, it seemed she forgot a lot of things.

"Did you know that she had a twin sister? Robyn, I think her name was?" Sara saw Abby stiffen when she mentioned the girl's name, whom Sara knew had tried to kill Abby.

Abby nodded. "Yes, but not at first. I mean…" Abby stopped and swallowed. "I mean, at first, I thought that it was my best friend, Megan though she was acting weird. Like when she didn't wait for me in the morning because we had always walked to school together. And that she didn't know where any of her classes were when we had been in school for almost two months."

Sara nodded, permitting Abby to continue.

"I knew Megan like the back of my hand, so I realized something was off about her. I didn't know what. So, I watched her and followed her out to the Tanner house one day after school. The day she tried to k… k… kill me," Abby stuttered. “And b…bury me in that hole in the woods,” Abby was shaking all over. “The moment she left me there, I ran. I ran as fast as I could away from her, and then I fell and must have blacked out or something. I remember little after that until I woke and came back to that house. The Tanner house to hide from her.

“So, you don’t recall when I found you lying in the road?”

Abby stared at her in confusion before shaking her head in denial.

“It was raining, and I saw you in the middle of the road. I pulled my car over to help you. You were still alive, but…” Sara stopped. Her mind reeling with flashes of that night. “You were wearing a pink coat.”

Abby shook her head. “I don’t own a pink coat.”

Chapter 41

Sara sat in her car, staring out the windshield. If it wasn't Abby she had seen that night, then who was it? That was the billion-dollar question she didn't have the answer to. Now, she felt stupid for asking Abby. She shouldn't, but she did. If Abby didn't own a pink coat, then who did? Sara didn't know that answer either. She had seen no one in town wearing a coat that fit that description. The fact was, if she had seen someone wearing that exact pink coat, she wouldn't be sitting here thinking about it. She wouldn't have talked to Abby. Well, yes, she would have still talked to Abby; she just wouldn't have asked her about that stupid coat she was so fascinated with. The coat that she swore she had seen that night—the one that had her searching and asking questions since she arrived here.

Her head felt foggy. She didn't even know how to find out if someone owned a pink coat. The only positive outcome from the conversation was that she had asked who Reece was and where she could find him. As for Megan, she was on a dead-end street. But that was where Reece came into the picture. At least she hoped.

She put the car in drive and drove into the central part of town. She parked the car at the curb, looked out the driver's side window, and saw Edith's house a few houses down the street. She didn't see any vehicles parked in the driveway from her vantage point or on the street at the curb. Were they done looking around? Not that she wanted to go back there and live. Not with everything that had happened in that house, with Edith and Steve being killed. No, she would stay at Delaney's house until she was told to leave, which would occur to her soon. That's if Officer Rosmus had anything to do with it, which she did.

She shook the thoughts from her head, not wanting to think about that woman right now—or ever, if she could help it. She grabbed the keys from the ignition, climbed out, and walked to the rear of the car. In front of her was the town grocery store, one she hadn't even stepped foot in since arriving here. She hadn't needed to.

She opened the door, and a bell *dinged* above her. She gazed around the store until her eyes fell on a man behind the counter. He was just as Abby had described him: tall, over six feet, with black, wavy hair that hung across his forehead.

She cleared her throat and strolled to the counter. "Hi, my name is…"

Reece cut her off. "I know who you are. Your name is Sara Nelson. You're from Bristol and a single child. You live with your grandmother, Ruth Nelson, and your mother is Teresa Nelson, who left when you were ten," Reece said, then continued. "You used to be the top of your class until you started dating Brad Griffin, whom you're hiding from. You're the girl who lived with Edith, and I had gotten you those transcripts so you could go to school here. Shall I continue?"

Sara stood with her mouth open, speechless. She thought she could come to this town and hide, that no one would know anything about her here. She believed she could start a new life, but that wasn't going to happen. She should turn around, get back in her car, and drive. Drive until she found a place where no one knew her and where Brad couldn't find her, but she knew that no such place existed. Reece knew everything about her, and Brad had found her here. How? She didn't know.

"Look, I have nothing against you. And I know that you didn't kill Edith or that guy Steve. Am I right?"

Sara nodded.

"Good, because I'm not usually wrong. I can uncover things that most people can't, but I won't delve into that with you. Why are you here? In my store?" Reece asked.

Sara swallowed. "I… I'm looking for information on Megan."

Reece narrowed his eyes at her and crossed his arms over his muscular chest. "What do you want with Megan?"

She felt scared and afraid of the man standing before her. Had she gone too far by asking questions she shouldn't be asking? Should she apologize and leave the store? Would he even let her leave after asking about Megan, whom he seemed to care deeply about? Maybe he was protecting her. Perhaps he knew where she was?

Sweat trickled above her brow. She rubbed her forehead with her hand and then wiped it on the back of her jeans. Her eyes shifted away from his. He made her feel weak and insecure. She needed time to think and figure out what to do next.

"I asked you, what do you want with Megan?" His voice grew louder.

Sara swallowed, feeling nauseous. *Just tell him what you know,* her mind quibbled. "I'm staying at her house and came across something that wasn't any of my business, and now

I'm wondering if she's okay?" Sara asked.

"What did you find?" he questioned, placing both hands on the counter. He leaned in toward Sara, as if she were about to reveal a secret.

Sara pulled out the necklace she had found and let it dangle between her fingers before them.

"Wait. She doesn't go anywhere without that necklace." Reece held out his hand.

Sara placed the chain in the palm of his large, calloused hand.

"It's broken?" Reece questioned.

Sara nodded.

"Where did you find this?"

"In a jewelry box in her bedroom," Sara replied.

"And?"

"And what?"

"I believe there's more than just the necklace that brought you here."

Now Sara knew why Megan had trusted this man and talked so much about him in her journal. "I found this in her room." She opened her purse and handed Reece the diary. "Turn to the page that's creased." She watched as he did this and looked back up at her.

"How do I know that I can trust you?" Reece asked.

"You don't," Sara replied. "Just as I don't know if I can trust you."

"Fair enough," Reece replied, then told her what had happened a few weeks ago and that both Delaney and Megan had left town. He mentioned that Megan didn't even say goodbye, which he thought was strange since they were very close.

"Kidnapping?" Sara asked. "Whoever she was talking about, or Megan herself, must have ripped the page out so no one could find it?"

Reece nodded.

Sara could tell that he knew more than he was letting on but also understood that he didn't trust her enough to share the whole truth. "Well, I think that Officer Rosmus is hiding something. She got angry when she caught me in Megan's room this morning."

"I'll look around and see what I can find out. Maybe I can find Megan and Delaney and make sure that they are all right."

"What do you want me to do?" Sara asked.

Keep searching that house. Perhaps Rosmus left a clue or something. Try to discover where they might have gone.

"You don't trust her either?" Sara asked.

"No."

She nodded. "Thanks for your help."

"No, thank you," he replied.

Sara started toward the door but then stopped and turned back around. "What do I do with this?" she asked, holding up the phone that Rosmus gave her.

"Who gave it to you?"

"Officer Rosmus."

Reece walked around the counter and stood in front of Sara. "That looks like Megan's phone," he said as he took it from Sara. "Do you have another phone you can use?"

"Yes."

"Good, use that phone and here," Reece said as he turned toward the counter, scribbled something down on a piece of paper, and handed it to Sara. "Here's my phone number. Call me anytime. If Rosmus is up to no good, then we will catch her."

"Okay," Sara said, taking the piece of paper and walking out the door. She climbed back into her car and drove away.

Chapter 42

She pulled into the driveway of Delaney's house and shut off the car. She opened the glove compartment and reached inside, pulling out her iPhone. She stared at it for the longest time, feeling nervous about turning it on. She knew what she had to do the moment she powered the phone back up: turn off the "find my phone." Though she understood it didn't matter, he had already found her.

She held down the power button, waiting for the white Apple logo to appear, but it didn't, which meant the phone was dead. Why did she think that turning off the phone and leaving it in the cold car would conserve the battery? Well, the truth was, she didn't give it much thought. She had other things going on in her life at that moment.

She grabbed the charger she had and climbed out of the car. Once inside the house, Sara walked to the bedroom where she was staying. She plugged her phone into the charger and then went back to the kitchen for something to eat.

She hadn't been in the house for five minutes before the front door opened and Officer Rosmus came stomping in. God, did that woman ever work? Was she watching Sara, and did she see her come home? This, she didn't know.

Sara stood in front of the microwave as Rosmus entered the kitchen. She didn't turn around or acknowledge the officer's presence in the room. She didn't need to.

"Where were you?" Officer Rosmus asked.

The Officer had been watching her. "I had to go to the store in town," Sara said, leaving out the part about talking to Abby.

Rosmus seemed to accept her answer, as she didn't have any further questions for Sara.

The microwave beeped, and Sara removed the plate of cooked pizza pockets she had found in the freezer. She grabbed a fork and sat down at the table. She wished the pizza pockets weren't steaming hot so she could shove one in her mouth. She didn't want to answer any more of the officer's questions because Sara knew Rosmus couldn't be trusted.

Officer Rosmus stood staring at Sara, then turned and walked back out the door without saying another word. Sara wondered why she had come here in the first place if she wasn't going to stay.

After Sara finished her food, she walked to the bedroom and grabbed her phone. She sat on the bed and powered it on. The white apple appeared. She placed her thumb on the home button to access the phone. She immediately went into her settings and turned off the app. She rolled her shoulders back and sat up straight to stretch her spine. The bones cracked along her spine, releasing the stress in the muscles.

It didn't dawn on her until just a second ago that no messages were appearing on the screen. No text messages or voicemails were on her phone. What did that mean exactly? Did her mother not care where she had disappeared to? Even her grandmother hadn't called her cell phone. But the one person she thought would call and text her hadn't, and that was Brad. There seemed to be nothing after she had opened her phone the last time. The night of the storm. What did that mean? He hadn't given up on her. This she knew to be true. No, he was hiding somewhere, waiting for the right moment to jump out and finish what he started back home.

She dug the piece of paper from the pocket of her jeans that Reece had given her and placed his number in her phone. There was only twenty percent battery life on her phone, so she left it plugged in while she did something else. But what else was there to do in this house?

Megan's room was off-limits. The door was now locked, though she could still try to find a way inside. And what about Delaney's bedroom? Reece had suggested looking for clues about where they might have gone.

Mail.

Sara didn't recall seeing any parcels sitting around. To be honest, that wouldn't be the first thing someone would think about. Would it?

She stood, left the bedroom, and walked back into the family room. She looked at the tables around the room but didn't see anything that resembled mail—no letters or magazines lying in a pile anywhere.

She entered the kitchen and looked around.

Nothing.

Then she searched through all the drawers in the kitchen but found nothing. There was no mail in the house, but that could mean Delaney had it forwarded to her new address.

Chapter 43

Sara sat up in bed, her head tilted toward the door. The sound was coming from somewhere in the house. That meant someone was in the house. Was it Officer Rosmus? Or had Brad found her? She didn't know and didn't want to leave the room to find out, but she couldn't stay here. She was being a 'fraidy cat, yet she had every reason to be. She wanted to stay because she knew she'd be safer here in this room.

She slipped out of bed and tiptoed to the door. She turned the lock on the knob and leaned her back against the wooden panels of the door. Then she pressed an ear to the door and listened. It sounded like someone was rummaging through the cabinets and drawers in the kitchen, but maybe it was happening in the bedroom? She wasn't certain.

She wondered if she should open the door to see who it was. Maybe if she startled them, they would run, or… would they kill her for seeing their faces? She didn't know what to do. Perhaps it was best to stay put and wait until they left, but what if they came to her room next? Then what would she do? She didn't have a weapon. Just as that thought crossed her mind, she gazed around the dark room.

She made her way to the window and opened the curtains to let in some light. The full, bright moon cascaded light throughout the room. A thought came to her that her grandmother had once told her: *"When the moon is full, that's when the crazies come out."* Sara thought it was ludicrous to believe something like that was true, but tonight, maybe her grandmother was right.

When she turned to look around the room, she spotted something behind the door. It was an aluminum cane. She wasn't sure how much damage the cane could do to a person, but she didn't see anything else she could use against the predator.

She gripped the cane in her right hand and stood behind the door. She heard footsteps moving down the hall and stopped just outside her door. She waited for the person to turn the knob, but they didn't. Instead, the footsteps receded. She heard a groan, possibly from the front door, which opened and then closed with a thud.

Sara's body sank to the floor. She hadn't realized she was shaking. She placed the cane beside her, pressing her hands flat onto the floor. Yet, that didn't stop her body from trembling. She pulled her knees to her chest and hugged them tightly, scared, but who wouldn't be after hearing someone in the house?

She was furious with herself for staying hidden in this room instead of confronting the person. But what if they had a gun or a knife? What was her small aluminum cane going to do against her attacker?

Sara pushed herself up from the floor and opened the bedroom door. She extended her hand and felt along the wall for the switch. When she found it, she flicked it on. Light filtered into the hallway.

She stepped out into the hall, cane in hand, and made her way toward the kitchen. Her eyes scanned the room but didn't see anything. Sara moved to the family room and saw nothing amiss. She had heard someone in the house, but the question was: what were they looking for?

She dashed back to the bedroom and picked up her phone. She dialed Reece's number.

x x x

Reece arrived at the house in under ten minutes. During that time, Sara changed her clothes and waited for him by the front door.

"Are you alright?" Reece asked.

"Yeah, I'm fine," she replied, but she wasn't fine. She was, in fact, scared to death.

She watched as Reece stepped into the room and walked toward the kitchen. "Stupid question, but do you have any idea what they may have been looking for?"

Sara shook her head. "Should I call Officer Rosmus and let her know that someone was in here?"

"Yes, and no. I believe that it was her," Reece said.

"But you won't tell me why you think it was her?" He didn't look at her, indicating that he wasn't going to share what he knew.

"I'll help you clean up."

"Okay, but I don't see how that will help solve who was in this house and did all this," Sara said as she gestured around the room.

"It will because you will text me the moment she arrives, and I will check out her house," Reece said.

Sara's eyes widened with surprise. "Oh," she said and smiled. "I take it you've done this before?"

Yes, it's a long story, but now isn't the right time to discuss it with you.

Sara nodded, feeling left with more questions than answers, she knew she wasn't going to get. Maybe she should follow Reece to see where this Officer Rosmus lived. She'd like to look around her house as well. Perhaps she'd find something that Reece missed?

Chapter 44

Hours later, when the sun came up, Sara woke and went into the kitchen. Officer Rosmus hadn't arrived yet, but once she did, Sara would follow Rosmus back to her house and wait until she left to search it. The hard part was that she had to stay invisible. Rosmus would see her car, especially in the daylight. So, how was she going to find out where the officer lived without being seen? She didn't know this, but she knew who she could ask.

Sara walked down the street and knocked on Abby's front door. Yesterday, when she followed Officer Rosmus to Delaney's house, she noticed that it was just down the road from Abby's house.

"Hi, I was wondering if Abby was here?" Sara asked Abby's mother, who stood in the doorway.

"I'm afraid she's not here. She went to school today. I told her that I didn't think it was a good idea, but she insisted," Abby's mother replied.

"Shit," Sara swore. She had forgotten all about school. But this was a good thing. Sara thanked Abby, left her house, jogged back to Delaney's, and climbed into her car. She arrived at the school within five minutes.

At lunchtime, she looked around for Abby. When she saw her, Sara walked to the table Abby was sitting at with her friends.

"Hey, Abby," Sara said. "Can I talk to you for a moment?"

Abby nodded and stood up, following Sara away from the table.

"I was wondering if you could tell me where Officer Rosmus lives?" Sara whispered. "But you can't say a word to anyone that I'm asking."

Abby appeared to study her for a moment before answering the question. "She lives at 1967 Kramer Road."

✢ ✢ ✢

Sara went to the library and found a map of all the streets in Craven Falls. She took a picture of the map with her cell phone. Excitement filled her. She had discovered the officer's house. It wasn't too far from Delaney's house. She'd simply walk there and hopefully be able to search the place.

Sara waited until it got dark, slipped out the back door of the house, and made her way along the wood line to Rosmus' house. She stood in the woods and scanned the house, noting that there were no lights on. Wondering if Rosmus was the type to go to bed early, she kept her vigil.

Well, the only way she would find out was by getting a closer look. She stayed near the trees and trotted toward the front of the house. She didn't see a vehicle in the driveway, and to her surprise, there was no garage either to park the vehicle in. This meant that Officer Rosmus wasn't home.

Sara smiled and ran to the side of the house. She inched her way along until she found a door. Reaching out, she turned the knob. It was unlocked. She tugged on the door, but it wouldn't budge. Stepping back, she threw her body weight against it. The door whipped open, and she fell inside.

She stood up and closed the door, leaning her back

against it as she regained her composure. She was sweating, her heart racing wildly beneath her chest.

Once she calmed down, she pulled her cell phone from her back pocket, turned on the flashlight app, and stepped further into the room. The place was empty; there was no furniture anywhere in the house. Had she gotten the address wrong? She moved through the small house, opening drawers and cabinet doors.

Nothing.

There was no way Officer Rosmus lived here, at least not anymore. After searching the entire house and finding nothing, she left.

Minutes later, she walked down the road toward Delaney's house. Seconds after her return, Officer Rosmus showed up.

"Oh, good, you're still up," Rosmus said.

Sara didn't say a word. Because she was afraid to speak, if she had been just a couple of minutes later, Rosmus would have seen her coming down the road. "Yeah, couldn't sleep," Sara replied. Then it hit her. This might be a good thing. Now she would wait for Rosmus to leave and then follow her to her new home. Though she would have to make sure she didn't follow too close.

* * *

Rosmus didn't stay for more than a few minutes, telling Sara she had to return to work. Sara waited until Rosmus drove down the road before leaving and getting into her car. She kept her headlights off as she followed.

Ten minutes later, Sara stopped her car in the road when she saw the officer pull into a driveway and then disappear into a garage. Sara would have to drive past the house, find a place to hide her car, and then walk back.

She wasn't sure how much time had passed while sitting hunkered down in the woods across the road from Officer Rosmus' house. Sara wouldn't claim to be a detective because she was far from it. In fact, this would be the first time she had ever staked out someone's house, waiting for them to leave. She just hoped that Rosmus wouldn't return too soon after she broke into her house.

Sara's eyes sprang open when she heard a garage door opening. She must have zoned out while watching the house. She shook her head. She wouldn't make a very good detective if she didn't pay attention on the job.

She rubbed her eyes and watched the vehicle back out of the driveway. She saw Officer Rosmus in the driver's seat as he turned onto the street and drove away.

"Okay, it's now or never," Sara mumbled.

She stood and ran to the tree line, looking around. She could see another house through the thick layer of trees on the left. No lights were on in the house, which meant that they were all sleeping.

Sara dashed across the road and up to the front yard. She tried the front door first, but it was locked. She peered through the windows but saw nothing, as there were no lights on inside. She skittered down the steps and made her way to the back of the house.

At the back door, she tried the knob, but it was locked once more. Did she genuinely believe it would be easy to get inside? That a police officer would leave the doors unlocked, particularly if they were hiding something?

Sara descended the stairs and tested all the windows along the back of the house.

Nothing.

They were all sealed tight.

She heard a noise and spun around. Without a flashlight and feeling too afraid to use the light from her cell phone in case someone saw her snooping around, she didn't see anything. Glancing back at the house, she almost missed the small window at ground level.

She jogged over to it and knelt on the frozen dirt. She pushed against the glass, and the window swung inward. She was sure that she could fit through the opening, but how was she going to get back out? She would most likely use the door when she left, but she'd figure that out later once she was inside.

She peeked in to get a look around. There was a table under the window on which she could place her feet. She turned and slipped her legs through the opening, dropping onto the table. The wooden surface wobbled under her weight. Quickly, she turned and jumped down to the cement floor below. She wouldn't be leaving the same way she came in.

She fished her phone from her coat pocket and turned on the flashlight. The room was small and empty, except for the table, which seemed odd and out of place. Maybe this was Rosmus' office? Though who in their right mind would have an office downstairs in the basement instead of on the first floor? Well, she didn't have to think hard about that answer. Look who she was talking about.

Sara pulled on the drawer. Locked. She moved on to the next drawer and found them all locked. Why would Rosmus lock all the drawers? Well, for one, to keep someone from finding something the officer didn't want them to find. Sara was sure few people, if any, came down into the basement searching through her desk, which they probably didn't even know was down here to begin with. The truth was, Rosmus technically wasn't supposed to be living here, right?

She walked to the only door in the room and opened it. She saw the stairs twenty feet in front of her but wanted to look around first before heading to the floor above. She moved her arm around, shining the light on everything in the room, but to her surprise, there was nothing. The place didn't look like most basements, which had scattered junk everywhere—things that people held onto, thinking that they would one day use them again, but then eventually sold or got rid of.

No, this part of the basement was empty. There were no racks or shelves with labeled boxes that held old photo albums or keepsakes. No washer, dryer, or even a freezer. The room was empty; not even a speck of dirt on the floor or a cobweb hanging from the ceiling.

Baffled by what she was seeing, she guessed that no one could truly know someone based solely on their appearance without understanding the way they lived. However, she hadn't gone upstairs, and she wasn't sure she wanted to.

The wooden boards creaked and moaned under the weight of her boots as she climbed the stairs to the main floor. She reached out and wrapped her hand around the cold metal doorknob. Her body trembled as she turned the knob, fearful of what she might find on the other side.

She opened the door and saw someone standing in front of her. It was dark, but she could tell that someone was there. Without thinking, she stepped back, lost her footing, and tumbled gracefully down the stairs while still holding onto the railing. By the time she reached the last step, her arm twisted, popping out of its socket as she hit the floor. Her tailbone struck the concrete floor. Pain shot up her spine before her head smacked the hard surface with a thud, and all went black…

Chapter 45

Sara felt excruciating pain throughout her entire body as if a freight train had hit her. She reached a hand to the back of her head and winced. There was a lump the size of an orange, and it was tender to the touch. It was the worst pain she'd ever experienced in her life. She squeezed her eyes shut, praying for the throbbing to subside, but it seemed to worsen.

She tried to move her left arm, but someone had secured it to the side of her body. She felt like a wrapped mummy, and her butt. Why did her butt hurt? She looked up and saw a white ceiling above her, one she hadn't noticed until now.

Where was she? She searched her mind for the events that had led her to this moment. She had been in Officer Rosmus' house, searching the basement. Her eyes widened as she remembered opening the door to the first floor and seeing a shadow—a figure standing in front of her—then she fell. She had fallen backward down the basement stairs and landed on the cement floor. Then she was here. But how? Who? Where the hell was she?

"Oh, good, you're awake," a woman said.

Sara turned her head to the side, which caused her additional pain. She saw an older woman sitting beside the bed, grateful that it wasn't Officer Rosmus. She didn't recognize this woman; she had never seen her before. Where was she? Who had taken her? How had she gotten here? She didn't know the answers to these questions and felt a bit nervous about finding out. Sara didn't feel scared because if this woman intended to hurt her or kill her, she would have done so already, wouldn't she? Besides, she was already in enough pain.

"Don't be afraid. You're in good hands here," said the woman. "My name is Catherine. Reece found you and brought you here."

"Reece," Sara whispered his name. She closed her eyes, letting the image of the figure in the doorway come to her. If she had positioned the light on her cell phone just enough to see the person's face, she would have seen that it was Reece standing there and not Officer Rosmus. Then she might not have stepped back and fallen down those stairs, hitting her head.

Catherine smiled at her again. "Would you like anything? Maybe more pain pills for your head and arm?"

"Yes, thank you."

"I'll be right back."

Sara watched Catherine leave the room and looked up at the ceiling again. She had heard no one enter the room.

"Hi," said a child's voice. "Are you a friend of my daddy's?"

Sara moved her gaze back to the spot where Catherine had been sitting moments before. She noticed a small child standing beside the bed, who had long, black, wavy hair like Reece's.

"Yes, I know your dad," Sara replied.

"I didn't ask if you knew him. I asked if you were a friend of his," the child corrected.

Sara wanted to laugh, but she knew that the jolting of her head would cause her too much pain. "Yes, I guess I am a friend of your daddy's."

The girl smiled at her.

"What is your name?" Sara asked.

"My name is Lily Rose Garran, and I'm eight and a half," Lily said, smiling, which made her eyes sparkle. "Since I told you my name, you should tell me your name. This way we won't be strangers. My mom said not to talk to strangers, but if I know your name, then you're not a stranger." Lily said matter-of-factly.

Sara wasn't sure it worked that way, but this little girl was smart; she had to give her that. "I'm Sara Nelson. I met your daddy at the grocery store in town."

Lily nodded. "Everyone knows my daddy works at the grocery store. Did you know he builds things too?" Lily smiled. "When summer comes, he will build me a treehouse. And one day, when my brother gets bigger, he will play in it too."

Sara smiled at this. She had never had a sibling, so she wouldn't know what it would be like to have one to do things with, such as playing in a treehouse.

"Maybe you can play in it with me?" Lily asked.

"Sure," Sara said, but she couldn't tell Lily she might not be around. Sara didn't know what would happen between now and next summer; Christmas hadn't even arrived yet.

"Lily Rose, what are you doing in here?" Catherine asked as she walked into the bedroom. "You need to get ready for school this instant."

"Yes, Grandma Cat," Lily said as she turned and walked to the door. She stopped and turned around. "Bye, Sara. It was nice to meet you."

"You too," Sara replied, but Lily had already skittered out of the room.

"I apologize for that. I hope she didn't cause you any trouble."

"No, not at all," Sara replied. "She's cute and smart, too."

"That she is. She'll have you eating out of the palm of your hand, that little one," Catherine said, a smile spreading across her face.

"Where's Reece?" Sara asked.

"He's downstairs eating breakfast. Do you want me to go get him?"

"No, I… I just wanted to…" Sara wasn't sure what she wanted to say to Reece. She was certain she didn't want to thank him for scaring the shit out of her and making her fall and smack her head on the floor. So, what could she possibly say to him? She didn't know, but she was confident he had some questions for her. Like, what was she doing in that house? Well, she would ask him that same question when she got the chance.

Catherine handed Sara two pills and helped her sit up so she could take them. Once Sara finished, she lay back down, grimacing.

"You rest, dear one, and I'll check in on you later," Catherine said.

Sara watched as Catherine walked out of the room, closing the door behind her. It hadn't been more than a few minutes, though she wasn't sure how much time had passed when the door creaked open again. She could hear heavy footsteps making their way to the side of the bed. She forced her heavy-lidded eyes open and saw Reece towering over her.

"It's good to see that you're awake," he said. "Now, tell me why you were in that house?"

Sara felt intimidated by him and swallowed. "I wanted to search the place," Sara replied, though her voice was slurred from the pain medication.

Reece nodded at her answer. "And what were you looking for? I thought I made it perfectly clear to stay out of this."

"Actually, you've never told me to stay out of whatever you think is going on. If you didn't know, I, without wanting to, was dragged into whatever the hell is going on in this town," Sara barked, causing her to cringe as a sharp pain spread across the top of her head.

Reece sat down in the chair beside the bed. "Look, I'm sorry that I scared you, and you got hurt. That wasn't my intention, but you shouldn't be snooping around in her house. Not because she's a police officer, but because you can't trust her."

Can't trust her? Sara questioned in her mind. "You know something about her, don't you?"

Reece nodded. "Look, I don't want you to get dragged into this."

"A little late for that, don't you think?" Sara muttered.

"I'm telling you to leave it alone. I will handle it."

Leave it alone? How can she just leave it alone? Edith and Steve are dead, and Mick ended up in the hospital. And he wanted her to pretend like nothing happened? That she might not be the cause of this when she was sure she was? That she is!

"I don't agree with you, but I'm in no shape to argue,"

Sara whispered. She would have to wait until her head felt better, then continue looking for answers.

"What about Officer Rosmus? She will wonder where I went since I'm not at Delaney's house. She'll be looking for me."

"I'll handle that. She won't know that you were in her house or that you're hurt. I will tell her that you felt safer staying with friends," Reece replied.

Sara wanted to laugh at his words, but that would only cause her more pain. Friends? She hadn't known Reece until yesterday. How could they be friends? Just because she had confided in him about Megan. Could she trust Reece? Though he had helped her so far, that meant nothing. She had no other choice; she wasn't in any shape to do anything. With her head, arm, and tailbone out of commission, she wasn't sure how long she'd be in bed. She'd have to stay here in his house and let her body heal before deciding what to do next.

Chapter 46

After two days in bed, Sara could finally walk around without causing herself more pain. After a week, she felt like herself again. She hadn't asked if she had fractured her skull or her tailbone, but if she had, she was sure that they would have taken her to the hospital, wouldn't they? This she didn't know. They seemed like a nice family, but could she trust them? She wasn't sure who in this town she could trust, but they hadn't done anything but take care of her since she ended up here in this house.

Sara grasped the banister as she descended the stairs into the kitchen. She spotted Catherine by the stove, stirring something in a large pot.

Catherine turned as Sara entered the room. "Oh, good. I'm so glad that you're up and moving around. Sit, I'll get you something to eat," Catherine said, as she placed the wooden spoon into a red ceramic spoon holder.

Sara pulled a chair out from the table and cautiously sat down, being careful not to sit on the center part of her butt. She should ask for a pillow to help soften the pressure, but she didn't want to bother the kind woman who had been taking care of her since they brought her here. Seconds later, she heard a noise coming from the monitor that was sitting on the counter.

"I'll be right back," Catherine said as she shuffled out of the room, returning with a baby on her hip. She placed the baby in the highchair at the end of the table. "This is Cole,

Ashley, and Reece's baby boy," Catherine said as she placed a handful of Cheerios on the tray in front of him.

Sara smiled at the baby, who was eyeing her. He smiled and giggled back at her. The baby grabbed a Cheerio and held it out for Sara to take.

"No, thank you. You eat it," Sara replied.

Without hesitation, the baby popped the cereal into his mouth, flashing her a toothless grin. Cole would smile at Sara and then shove another piece into his mouth along with half of his fist. Sara grinned at this. *Babies were so innocent without a care in the world,* she thought. And wondered if she had been just like this baby. She couldn't recall any of her childhood, though most people can't. Not until they were at least four or five years old.

Several minutes later, Catherine placed a plate on the table in front of Sara, containing scrambled eggs, bacon, and a slice of buttered toast. Her mouth watered as the scent wafted up and into her nose. She took a bite of the eggs, realizing she hadn't tasted anything this good in a long time—well, since Edith's cooking.

Catherine said, "I guess you were hungry."

Sara nodded while she continued to eat the meal that had been cooked for her. Several minutes later, she scooted her chair back, stood up, and walked her plate to the sink to wash it.

"Oh, no you don't," Catherine said as she stepped in front of Sara. "I'll clean that for you."

"I'm sure I can handle cleaning my plate. It's the least I can do since you're allowing me to stay here in your home."

"Nonsense," Catherine replied, taking the plate from Sara's hand.

"Well, thank you. Though I don't expect you to wait on me hand and foot. I'm feeling better," Sara stated.

"I'm sure you are, but you're a guest in my home, and I will take care of you."

Sara smiled at this, but still felt like she was taking advantage of this kind woman. "Let me know if there's anything I can do to help you."

"Just sit and relax; I'll take care of things," Catherine said as she turned around and placed the plate into the soapy water.

Sara did just that. She sat down next to baby Cole, who had finished all his food.

"Do you want more?" Sara asked Cole.

The baby laughed as he bobbed his head up and down.

Sara reached over and poured more cereal onto his tray. He grabbed a fistful, opened his mouth as wide as possible, and stuffed his small, round fist of Cheerios into his mouth.

"Cole," Catherine said beside him. "One at a time. You'll choke if you shove them all into your mouth."

As if he understood, Cole removed his hand from his mouth, emptied all the pieces onto the tray, and grabbed one piece with his chubby fingers. He held it up to show his grandma before placing it in his mouth.

"That's better," Catherine said, walking away.

* * *

Later that afternoon, after Sara had lain back down for a nap, she woke when she heard a loud vehicle outside. Someone was revving their car engine. She slipped out from under the covers and made her way to the window to see who was making all that commotion. Through the woods, she saw an SUV sitting in a driveway that looked awfully like the truck Officer Rosmus drove. Though she couldn't be certain, as the trees shielded part of the vehicle, it would explain how Reece knew that Sara had been in her house.

Her gaze left the vehicle and traced the scenery. It was the first time Sara had looked outside, and to her surprise, it had snowed. Winter had finally arrived. Sara didn't seem thrilled by this, but knew it would snow eventually. The cold made her shiver, and she stepped away from the window as if shocked by an electric current.

She rubbed her hands up and down her arms, but she couldn't seem to shake the chill coursing through her body. She turned around, grabbed a sweater lying at the foot of the bed, and put it on. Catherine must have come into the room and left it for her while she was sleeping. The pain pills had knocked her out because she had never heard the door open or anyone enter the room.

She opened the bedroom door and walked into the bathroom across the hall. After finishing, she was about to go down the stairs when she heard someone talking.

"Ashley, listen. She's not a threat to our family. Trust me on this," Reece said.

"I do trust you, but I don't know her. She was in that house, Reece, when they found those two bodies. How do you know she wasn't the one who killed them? She showed up here, and more people started dying," Ashley countered.

"Because I know she didn't do it. Someone is doing this to her, and I'm going to figure out what's happening! I promise you with my life that I won't let anything happen to you or our family again," Reece said.

Everything went quiet downstairs, and Sara wondered if it was her cue to head down the stairs and make herself known, but she didn't budge. She wanted to wait until she heard the two of them walk away and enter the kitchen, but no one seemed to move or make a sound.

Sara stepped down onto the wooden step, then the next. She prayed they wouldn't hear her coming, that the wood wouldn't creak under her weight and give her away.

She knew that if she took two more steps down, she would be past the wall, and if they were in the living room, they would see her. So, she stopped and listened.

"Do you think that Crystal's involved again?" Ashley asked. "After what happened last month?"

Sara leaned forward, listening for Reece to respond, but she didn't hear anything. This meant he was either not going to answer the question or he had nodded.

"Hi," said a little voice from behind her.

Sara glanced over her shoulder and saw Lily standing on the landing behind her, holding a doll. Just as Sara was about to turn and head back up the stairs to hush the girl, she heard a noise at the bottom of the stairs and turned to see Reece staring back at her.

Chapter 47

"I'll just leave," Sara said as she stood in the bedroom where she was staying.

"No, you're still healing," Reece replied.

She knew he still felt guilty for making her fall and hit her head. "I'll be fine. I don't want your family in danger because of me."

"They're not in danger. I can take care of them," Reece replied. "Don't worry about my family. Besides, it's you that I'm worried about."

"Is Ashley, right? Is Officer Rosmus someone I should be afraid of? Do you think she's behind all of this?"

Reece looked into Sara's eyes and nodded.

"Oh, hell," Sara mumbled before slapping a hand over her mouth. She had forgotten that Lily was in the next room and could probably hear them talking. "What did I get myself into?"

"Look, I think you're safer if you stay here."

"No, I can't. Not if I'm the one putting your family in harm's way," Sara said, pointing down at the floor. She liked Reece's family and didn't want anyone to get hurt or worse—killed. She wouldn't be able to live with herself if something terrible happened to these nice, caring people who took her in when they didn't have to.

"Look, I know I can't make you stay here, but you should. I can protect you," Reece said.

Sara studied his face. She knew he was right. She would be safer here than anywhere else, but she understood she shouldn't stay. Yes, she could keep an eye on Officer Rosmus from her room. Well, maybe? And she needed to have her head healed before she left, but… There was always a "but." She was leaving, regardless of whether Reece agreed. Even if she had to sneak out in the middle of the night, she doubted that was a possibility with him in this house. He would hear her leave and follow her. Had that been how he knew she was in Rosmus's house? Had he been watching and seen Sara go in through the window? She believed this to be true and didn't dare let the words leave her mouth. Reece seemed to know everything that happened in this town.

Sara looked at him. Yes, she was sure that he had been in the military and probably in special forces, she assumed. "Okay, fine. I'll stay for now." She would devise a plan to leave this town as soon as possible, before Brad came for her.

"Thank you, Sara." With those final words, Reece turned, opened the bedroom door, walked out, and went down the stairs.

The mattress springs squeaked as Sara sat down on the bed, feeling defeated. She knew she couldn't stay here, but where else could she go? Certainly not back to Delaney's, even though all her things were there. Maybe she would send Reece to get them for her? Yes, that was a possibility because she didn't want to come face-to-face with Officer Rosmus if she didn't have to.

Sara remained silent at the dinner table as she listened to the family discuss their day. She felt sad because she had never experienced a family like this. They had never sat down and talked about their day or whatever was on their minds. That's when she realized she couldn't let them get hurt because of her. Tomorrow, she was leaving, and there was nothing anyone could do to stop her.

✢ ✢ ✢

The next morning, Sara waited until Ashley, Lily, and Reece had left the house. She was relieved that she didn't need to take anything with her other than the clothes on her back. As she made her way down the stairs, she could hear Catherine in the kitchen talking to baby Cole.

Sara glanced at the front door as she descended the last two steps. She paused, looked toward the kitchen, and then back to the front door. This was her moment to leave. Catherine was preoccupied with the baby; she could slip out, and no one would notice.

She grabbed her coat hanging on the hook by the door and put it on, then shoved her feet into her boots. She glanced over her shoulder to see if Catherine was watching her, but there was no one. She twisted back around, unlocked the deadbolt with one hand and turned the knob with the other. A cold breeze swept in, cutting through the fabric of her coat. She shivered and stepped back from the door while still holding onto the doorknob.

She pushed open the screen door, which squeaked. Turning, she looked over her shoulder again. No one emerged from the kitchen; the coast was clear.

She stepped onto the porch and closed the door behind her, followed by the screen door. The snow that had covered the ground yesterday had vanished, leaving no trace of winter behind. She bounded down the steps, crossed the side yard, and ventured into the woods next to the house. While the trees wouldn't provide much cover, it was better than being out in the open.

When she stepped into the woods, she turned toward the house; Catherine hadn't heard her leave. She wasn't at the door, and Sara didn't see her by any of the windows either. Then, she heard a noise from behind her and turned back around, facing Officer Rosmus's house. The officer was doing something in the garage, but Sara couldn't see from where she stood.

She crouched down behind a thick layer of branches. A rabbit peered out as if to indicate that this was his home. Then the rabbit darted out from underneath the brush and ran toward the road.

She heard something slam shut, and then Officer Rosmus came stomping out of the garage in her heavy combat boots. She opened the truck door and climbed inside. The garage door lowered to the ground as the truck backed out of the driveway and onto the street. Officer Rosmus drove in the opposite direction, away from town.

Sara looked back at Officer Rosmus's house and noticed that the garage door hadn't closed completely. It had stopped precisely a foot from the ground. Could this be a sign for her to continue the search inside the house?

Without wasting another minute, Sara ran to the house and rolled under the garage door. Once on the other side, she stood up and took her cell phone from her coat pocket, shining the light around the room. Aside from the usual items found in a garage like metal shelves, tools, boxes, plastic tubs, and a freezer, everything looked normal.

Sara moved around the room, searching for anything

unusual or concealed from plain view. When she reached the freezer against the wall, she noticed something uncommon for freezers: a padlock fastened to the freezer door.

Sara reached out and lifted the lock. It wasn't fastened. Fear stirred in her stomach. Why would there be a lock on the freezer? *To keep someone from looking inside, of course. Or to keep someone from getting out,* Sara pondered.

She unfastened the lock and removed it. Taking a deep breath, she exhaled and lifted the freezer door.

Chapter 48

The lock fell from her hand and hit the cement floor, echoing off the walls. She covered her mouth with her hand to muffle the scream rising from her throat. If she let the sound escape, it would alarm the neighbors, though the only one close enough to hear would be Catherine next door. Perhaps she should scream and create a scene because someone else needed to see what was inside the freezer.

Sara was certain that it wouldn't have bothered her if there had been a deer in the freezer, but there wasn't. There was a body in the freezer—one she knew all too well.

The body was Brad's.

He stared up at her, those same eyes haunting her in her dreams.

He was dead!

Sara's hand dropped from her mouth, her body shaking all over. She thought she might feel sick, but she didn't. She didn't feel sorry for him or sad about his death. Although bile rose in her throat, she swallowed the nasty, acidic bitterness back down. It burned as it returned to her stomach, where it belonged.

Questions formed in her head. How long had he been dead? How long had he been in this freezer? Was it before or after Edith's and Steve's deaths? Or when Mick said she saw someone in the house before she ran out the back door and into the woods? This, she didn't know. She wasn't even sure how to determine how long someone had been dead when frozen. She was sure the medical examiner checked a dead person's temperature by inserting a thermometer into their liver. But she didn't have a person like that around, and she wasn't about to call one. She wasn't going to call anyone. Besides, what good would it do? He was already dead. Though it would answer the questions that had been troubling her.

Sara hadn't realized she was crying until a tear fell from her cheek to the floor. Yes, Brad had once meant something to her, but did he deserve to die? Yes and no. People who have killed others, as Brad had, deserve to die.

Before closing the freezer door, Sara decided to take a video of the garage and what she had found. When she finished, she placed the lock back on the freezer just as she had found it. Then she walked to the door and went inside the house. She kept the recorder running to film everything. She needed all the evidence she could gather to put this bitch behind bars.

She entered the kitchen, which looked immaculate. She knew this from her time in the basement, where Officer Rosmus had shown herself to be a bit of a neat freak. She moved the iPhone around the room before continuing through the rest of the house.

In the hall, she encountered a closed door. Sara twisted the knob and pushed the door open. She saw a small bed, perfectly made. The room was tidy and appeared as though no one had ever slept inside.

Sara walked over to the dresser and opened the drawer. It was empty. She moved on to the next one. There were no clothes or personal items inside any of the drawers. She opened another door that looked like a closet. No clothes hung on the hangers. She didn't even see a dust bunny rolling around on the floor. The place was spotless. She left the bedroom and walked to the next door, which led to the bathroom. She filmed the contents of the cabinets and left the room.

The next room was another bedroom, also immaculate. Sara rummaged through the drawers and found clothing this time. *This must be Officer Rosmus's bedroom,* she thought. She checked under everything but made sure not to disturb the neatly folded garments.

In the closet, she saw boxes stacked one on top of the other. Labeled **"Family Pictures,"** some had no writing on them. Sara reached up, grabbed a green-flowered box, and placed it on the bed. She removed the lid and shuffled through the photos. She had no idea who she was looking at. While she recognized some pictures of Megan, she was certain the other girl in the photo, though younger and seemingly deceased, was Robyn. She had no clear idea what she was searching for.

Her hand stopped when she saw a picture of a cabin. She held the photo out while still filming. It looked like any other cabin she had seen during summers at Lake Erie with her friends. Maybe this had been photographed near a lake as well? Although the picture seemed taken from afar, that didn't mean there wasn't a lake nearby.

She placed the picture back in the box and repositioned the lid before returning it to the closet, exactly where she had found it. After finishing her search of the room, she made her way back toward the kitchen where she had started.

Her ears perked up when she heard a vehicle approaching down the road. The sound was familiar to her.

Officer Rosmus was back, which meant two things. First, she hadn't driven too far away from wherever she had gone, and second, Sara needed to get out of the house—and fast!

She didn't have time, nor could she escape back through the open garage door. Her only option was to go out the back door and into the woods. And that's exactly what she did. But when she reached the tree line behind the house, she remembered that she had forgotten to lock the back door. The back door looked splintered around the frame, as if someone had recently attempted to break into the house. Well, there was nothing she could do about it now. Besides, Officer Rosmus would probably think that she had just forgotten to lock it before leaving the house earlier. At least that's what Sara hoped she would think. Sara wasn't planning on sticking around to find out either.

She navigated through the woods until she reached a creek. She recognized it had to be the same creek that flowed beneath the bridge she had crossed when arriving in town weeks prior.

She walked over to a large rock and sat down. She needed to rest for a few minutes because her head was pounding from all the blood pumping through her body. Then, she would continue walking until she found her car, which she suddenly realized was in the opposite direction from where she was. She would just have to hide out here until nightfall. Then, she would head back to the main road, get into her car, and drive away.

She wouldn't even stop to grab her things at Delaney's house. She didn't care at all. All she knew was that she had to get out of this town before she ended up dead like the people she cared about. But she understood that she couldn't leave until she figured out what Officer Rosmus was up to. What was she hiding? And why did she have Sara's ex-boyfriend inside the freezer in her garage?

Clearly, Rosmus had killed him, right? What other reason could she have for keeping him in the freezer? Sara realized then that Rosmus had also killed Steve and Edith too. She just didn't know why.

Chapter 49

Sara stood and climbed the small hill as the sun sank below the trees. Night would arrive soon, and she needed to find her way out of the woods before it got too dark. She didn't want to leave the safe haven the creek offered, as she listened to the rushing water, but she couldn't stay. She considered following the flow of the water and where it might lead. But what good would that do if she got lost? Not only was she on foot, but it was freezing outside. Besides, she had to return and get her grandmother's car.

She found what appeared to be a path at the top of the hill and followed it. Ahead, she could see the back of a house. The lights were on, and she noticed people moving around through the standard-size window. Inside, a person stopped, and she realized it was Reece.

"Shit!" she muttered. She couldn't seem to get away from him. She would just have to stay put until they went to bed before she could sneak out of the woods and onto the road.

Every few minutes, a cool breeze nipped at her face and drifted down, slipping under her thick coat and making her shiver. She sank to the ground, hugging her knees to her chest to keep warm. Not that it was working, but what else could she do? Standing made her colder. She couldn't very well build a fire, which would definitely give her away.

She wasn't sure how long she had been sitting under the tree when she heard a door screech open. She looked up toward Reece's house. No one was there. That left Officer Rosmus's house because there were no other homes nearby. At least none that she could see.

She couldn't see much from her seat, and she didn't want to stand up, fearing that whoever was outside would spot her. She listened and waited for someone to come into her line of sight, but no one appeared.

She pulled her phone from her pocket and looked at the time. She had forgotten that with winter came early sunsets. Her cell phone read 4:24 p.m. She would make her way to the front of the house soon. There was no way she could stay here until they all went to bed. She'd freeze to death before that happened.

As she walked several feet into the tree line beside Reece's house, she scanned the roof peak for any signs of a motion detector. She didn't see any but also knew that she had to be within a certain distance to trigger one if it existed. When she reached the road, she looked around before crossing. She would need to hide in the trees as she passed the officer's house.

Chains rattled as the garage door lifted. Officer Rosmus was on the move again. Sara ducked down behind a fallen tree as the officer backed out of the driveway and drove past her. Sara needed to follow her, but how? She was on foot.

Once the taillights vanished, Sara headed to the road and began jogging toward where she had hidden her car.

She stopped at the back of her car to catch her breath before getting behind the wheel. The cold air stung her lungs. She pressed a hand to her chest, helping herself to slow her breathing. Once she felt better and was no longer dizzy, she climbed into her vehicle.

The engine roared to life, despite having sat in the woods for what, a week? Well, it didn't really matter. This car could withstand anything and still start. She sat, allowing the car to warm up as she pondered how to turn it around. She didn't want to back out onto the road, in case Rosmus returned and spotted her.

Sara drove straight down the dirt road, thinking she would look for a turnabout or access to another road. She planned to head in the same direction as Officer Rosmus had gone, but what would she do if she passed Officer Rosmus driving and noticed her? She decided to worry about that when it happened; besides, it was dark now, so the chances of being seen were slim.

Sara kept her speed to a crawl because of all the ruts in the road when she spotted a road up ahead. She slowed to a stop, looking in both directions. She needed to decide which way to turn: left or right? She thought about the dirt road she was on now and realized she didn't recall any curves in it. This meant that if she went left, she would head back into town. If she turned right, she would go in the direction that Rosmus had driven, and they would meet somewhere in the middle. The thing was, she had no clue if the roads connected. If it were actually one road, then she would go in a complete circle, *wouldn't she?*

Without hesitation, she turned right.

A few minutes later, she slammed on the brakes, causing her body to lurch forward in her seat. She noticed a pair of headlights in the woods to her left. They weren't moving, which meant the vehicle was parked. The lights faced away from the road she was on. She could tell it wasn't a car because the lights were much higher off the ground, like a pickup truck, unlike her car that sat low. She recognized all this from the position of the headlights. Did that mean Officer Rosmus was out there? And if so, what was she doing?

An idea struck her. She would return the way she came and park the car. Then she would head into the woods to see if she could uncover what Rosmus was up to. Images of the officer burying a body flashed in her mind. Brad's body? She shook the thoughts away, but the images lingered at the forefront of her mind. She would never be able to unsee Brad's lifeless, frozen body inside that freezer.

Sara hadn't thought of a plan when she walked into the woods a few minutes later toward the truck with its headlights beaming. Dried leaves and dead branches covered the forest floor. She had to be careful not to step on them, but she couldn't see where she was walking. Well, at least not very well. There was some light from the moon, but the trees seemed to obscure most of it. God, she wished she could use her cell phone.

She froze when a branch cracked beneath her boot. Her eyes darted quickly over the surrounding scenery.

Nothing.

She didn't see or hear anything, which meant that no one had heard her.

She took another step forward and then stopped beside a massive walnut tree. She recognized this by the tree's enormous trunk and the numerous branches that spread out above her head. If necessary, she would climb the tree to hide, and it would also provide her with a better view of her surroundings.

She heard a door creak open, and it wasn't coming from

the truck. She was sure of that. Why did it have to be so freaking dark out here in these woods? Again, she wished she could use her cell phone to see, but that would be a stupid move. The person would catch her, and who knew what this person out here would do to her? If it were Officer Rosmus, which she was positive it was, she would probably throw Sara into the back of her SUV and haul her into town. Throw her in a jail cell for—for what, being in these woods? For trespassing? Or kill her like she did Brad? No one would come looking for her. They would think that Sara had just left town.

She would have to stay put and see what this person would do. Maybe she'd catch a glimpse of their face once they stepped into the light. Just as she thought it, the person approached the vehicle, their heavy footfalls snapping twigs as they made their way over. There was no doubt that the person was Officer Rosmus.

Sara couldn't mistake her face or build for anyone else's. But the question was, what was she doing out here? And what was in that building she had come out of?

Chapter 50

The truck lurched forward, weaving between the wide-open trees as Rosmus made her way to the road. The tires squealed when the vehicle hit the pavement, and she drove away.

Sara turned back toward the area where the officer had emerged. This time, she pulled out her phone, and light filtered around her. She still couldn't see far in front of her. She stepped away from the tree and walked forward until she could see the outer walls of a building. She was certain it was the cabin from the photo she had found in Rosmus's house, but she would have to wait until daylight to confirm what she already knew.

She trudged forward until she arrived at some wooden steps. With a hesitant move, she placed her foot on the first board. Her boot slipped, causing her to fall backward, but she caught herself with the banister and stood on solid ground. She shined the light down and saw the wood covered in green moss.

She grabbed the handrail and took her time walking up the steps. Once she reached the porch, she moved her phone's light around to get a better look. A window stood to the right of the door. She stepped closer to the window and shined the light inside. There was a small kitchen with a table and chairs. It looked just as clean as Rosmus's house did, which shouldn't surprise her, but it did. She swept the light across the room and saw a fully furnished living room.

Excitement surged through her as the thought of escaping the cold night air crossed her mind.

She stepped back to the door and turned the knob. Had she truly believed that the door would be unlocked? This was Officer Rosmus she was dealing with. And she was hiding something in this house. Sara could feel it.

She shone the light around the porch, searching for anything that could conceal a key. There was nothing—no mat or flowerpot, not even any furniture.

Nothing.

However, she hadn't checked above the door or the windowsill. That's exactly what she did. But again, there was no key. She even tried lifting the window, but it too was locked.

She knew that if she broke the window, Rosmus would immediately notice when she returned to the house. Sara was sure she would come back, but for what reason? What was it that the officer kept coming to the cabin for? Sara had seen nothing inside, but that didn't mean there wasn't something in the rest of the house that she couldn't see from the window. She was certain there were bedrooms inside—rooms that hid secrets from the residents of Craven Falls. She already knew that Crystal Rosmus wasn't who she pretended to be, and Sara wouldn't leave until she uncovered the truth. The truth that Officer Rosmus was a killer!

Sara left the porch and walked around the side of the cabin. The windows on this side of the house were all too high. She wouldn't be able to see inside, let alone reach them to check if they were unlocked. Who in their right mind would place a window so high off the ground?

She continued around the house, searching for a way in. Maybe there was a basement like at Rosmus's house, and she could crawl through a window? She scanned the ground level but found nothing. She was getting nowhere, and the temperature outside was dropping—fast. She needed to get warm. If she didn't find a way in soon, she would have to head back to her car for the night. She had checked every inch of the ground around the cabin and realized that she wasn't getting into this house. Not tonight, anyway.

Tomorrow, she would explore the surrounding area to see what she could find. In the daylight, she would notice things that she couldn't see at night.

Chapter 51

Behind closed eyes, she felt the morning light streaming through the car windows. The sun warmed her, but not enough to chase away the cold shivers. Part of her wanted to lie there and sleep, forgetting about the world around her. But she knew she needed to figure out her next move. Like going back to that cabin and finding a way inside. She was certain someone was in there—something that kept Officer Rosmus returning, and Sara would find out what.

She opened her eyes and sat up. The backseat wasn't uncomfortable, but it wasn't comfortable either. The leather seats felt hard, as if she were sleeping on a wooden floor, and she had only one blanket. Sure, she could have slept in the front seat and started the car from time to time, but she didn't want to waste gas.

She also considered simply leaving town, but she couldn't go after discovering Brad's body in that freezer. She needed to solve the mystery that brought her here. She could talk to Reece, but she didn't want to involve him and his family. She didn't want any of them to get hurt or, worse, killed.

Just like Edith, Steve, and Brad.

Too many people she was in contact with were getting hurt or killed. She had thought it was Brad; sure, he could have killed both Edith and Steve, but finding Brad's body inside that freezer indicated to her that he wasn't the one who had committed those terrible acts, not that he wasn't capable. She had seen him firsthand, beating her friend Jay back in Bristol, all because of jealousy.

A thought struck her. She was convinced that Officer Rosmus might be the one who killed Edith and Steve. Was she possibly the person in the house when Mick was there? Or could it have been Brad? She had pondered this same question before when she discovered Brad dead, and still, she found herself without answers. The only certainty she held was that she couldn't leave until she uncovered the truth.

There were actually three things left for her to do. First, figure out what Officer Rosmus was hiding in that cabin. Second, who had killed Edith and Steve? Third, who was the girl she had seen on the road when she arrived? Because Abby said she didn't own a pink coat, and Robyn, the girl in the hole she found in the woods, had been wearing a red coat. Aubrey was wearing a black coat, so that left someone else, but who?

She crawled over the seat and sat behind the wheel of the car. She inserted the key into the ignition and started the engine. It took almost fifteen minutes for the car to fill with heat. She placed her hands in front of the vent. The heat poured out, and she relaxed against the seat. Yet, she hadn't realized how tense she had been or how her muscles hurt and burned beneath her skin.

Her stomach growled. She hadn't eaten in two days and had nothing to drink. If she didn't eat or drink soon, she would be dead. She decided to first go to Delaney's to grab her things. Then she would head to the café to get something to eat.

As she drove into town, she realized she had completely forgotten about school. There was so much happening in her life. She thought of Mick and wondered how she was doing and whether she was still in the hospital, which she doubted. Maybe she would stop by her house after grabbing something to eat and check on her.

The thing was, she didn't know where Mick lived. She had never been to his house and was never invited over. Mick had always come to Edith's house, so Sara had no clue where Mick lived. Maybe she would ask around at the café. Someone there had to know, but would they tell her? This she didn't know, but she would find out; besides, there was always Reece at the grocery store across from the diner.

The moment she walked into the café, everyone seemed to glance in her direction. Had it been a mistake for her to come here? She would simply have to ignore their stares and pretend they weren't looking at her. And that's exactly what she did as she found an empty booth in the back of the café.

"Glad to see that you're doing fine?" said a male voice.

Sara looked up and saw Mr. Waters, the owner, standing beside the table. She had forgotten all about her job at the café, which was the same day that Steve showed up. Then Edith died and they found Steve's body. It was all so crazy.

"Uh, yeah. I'm so sorry," Sara said.

"No need to explain. I just hadn't heard from you and wanted to make sure that you were okay. You know, with what happened with Edith and all."

She nodded. "Yes, I'm…" She had to lie to him because saying she wasn't fine would only create more questions, and she couldn't have people asking her questions that she didn't have the answers to. "I'm fine," she replied.

"Well, your job is still available if you want it," Mr. Waters said before turning and walking away.

Sara nodded, but she doubted that Mr. Waters had seen her. It seemed he was busy waiting tables, which meant that Mick hadn't returned to work yet, or that she was at school.

The bell *dinged.*

Sara glanced at the door and made eye contact with Officer Rosmus.

Chapter 52

They stared at each other for a few moments before Sara looked down at the table. She could still feel the officer's eyes on her until Rosmus finally turned away and took a seat at the counter. Sara stood up and moved to the opposite side of the booth, away from Rosmus's beady eyes.

Sara ordered food and sipped her glass of water while waiting for her meal. After eating, she paid her bill and slipped out of the café. She crossed the street, walked down the sidewalk, and entered the grocery store.

Once inside, she closed her eyes as if to steal a few seconds of silence before facing the one person who had been helping her before she ditched him and took matters into her own hands. Not that she was doing anything yet, but she would sort out this little mystery and show Craven Falls who Officer Rosmus really was—a murderer.

Reece stood behind the counter. Their eyes met, but no words were spoken. Sara moved toward the counter, facing two options. One, she could tell him about the cabin in the woods and what she saw last night in Rosmus' garage. Or two, she could keep it to herself. But then why was she here in his store if she wasn't going to involve him? Well, because she wanted to know where Mick lived so she could check on her and ensure that she was okay before heading back to that cabin, just in case it would be the last time they ever saw one another.

"Hey," Reece said.

She nodded in response. She wasn't sure what she could or should say to him after leaving his house without saying goodbye. What was there to say?

"How's the head?"

Well, that wouldn't have been her first question to someone who had sneaked out of their home. Did that mean he cared about what happened to her? Yes, he cared about her; otherwise, why would he have taken her into his home?

Given everything that's happened lately, she had forgotten about hitting her head, which she considered a good sign. She lifted a hand and touched the spot where she had felt the medium-sized lump a week ago, which had now shrunk to the size of a grape.

"I'm fine. Thank you for asking."

Reece didn't acknowledge her response, not even with a nod.

Her hand dropped to her side as she walked closer to the counter. "I was wondering if you could tell me where Mick lives. I'd like to see how she's doing."

Reece seemed to study her as if she were about to pull out a knife and slice his throat with it. Didn't he know he could trust her? Although she hadn't given him any reason to, had she? She left without telling him where she was going, and he was probably worried about her. She hadn't even left him a note.

But that seemed to be her thing these days: running away from all the problems she didn't want to face, even the good things that had happened. Lately, though, it seemed hard to tell the difference between the two because everything appeared to be falling apart.

"She lives around the corner, about half a mile, in apartment building 2. Her apartment is 202B."

Sara hadn't known there were apartments here in Craven Falls. She also hadn't gone looking for them. Honestly, this shouldn't surprise her; Craven Falls always seemed to have something lurking around every corner.

"Thank you," she said and left the store without another word. The moment she stepped outside, she knew she should go back inside and apologize to him.

But she didn't. She couldn't. She needed to keep Reece out of this mess. Not for him, because he could take care of himself, but for his family because they didn't deserve anything bad to happen to them. In fact, Sara loved his family. They were kind and caring. And they didn't have to take her into their home when Ashley hadn't wanted her there.

She walked back to her car and drove around the corner. A half-mile down the road, the apartment buildings came into view. Craven Falls didn't seem like the kind of town that would have apartments, but neither did Bristol, where she had come from. Back in her hometown, there were plenty of places to rent and live.

Sara spotted Building 2 and parked the car. Seconds later, she stood outside in front of a locked glass door. She searched for Mick's name on the keypad, then remembered that the last name would be listed, not the first name. There in the second row was the name Thurman. She pressed the button and waited.

"Hello," crackled a woman's voice.

"Hi, it's Sara. Is Mick home?"

"Sara? Is that you?"

Sara recognized the voice once the crackling noise stopped. "Mick, hey. Yes, it's me, Sara. Can I come in?"

A moment later, she heard a buzzing sound and opened the door. She walked up the stairs to the second floor and found Mick waiting for her outside the door.

"How are you feeling?" Sara asked.

Mick enveloped Sara in his arms without answering. The gesture surprised Sara, but she also wrapped her arms around Mick. When they released each other, Mick turned and went inside the apartment, while Sara followed, closing the door behind her.

"When did you get out of the hospital?" Sara asked.

"Mabel brought me home last week."

"Oh," Sara said, looking around for Mabel but not seeing or hearing her in the apartment.

"She isn't home right now. She got called into work," Mick replied before Sara had a chance to speak. "You just missed Officer Rosmus, too."

Sara felt her eyes widen as her mind raced through every scenario for why the officer had come to Mick's house. Maybe she was just checking to ensure that Mick hadn't seen her in the house that night? Yes, that seemed plausible. Or perhaps she genuinely cared and wanted to make sure Mick was doing okay since her return from the hospital, but Sara had her doubts. Not after what she had found in that freezer.

"What did she want?" Sara asked.

Sara walked over to the sofa and sat down, waiting for Mick to do the same, but she didn't. Instead, she just stood there, staring at the wall behind Sara as if she were in a trance. "Mick, are you okay?" Sara asked, but Mick didn't respond.

Sara stood and rushed over to where Mick was standing, placing a hand on each of her arms. She could feel Mick trembling under her touch. She wasn't sure if Mick was having a seizure, but she had seen how people react during one. Mick wasn't shaking compulsively like those people do; her eyes weren't rolling into the back of her head. The only logical conclusion seemed to be that Mick was still frightened after what had happened to her. As she should be. No one would come back from what she had experienced without some kind of trauma, especially when that person who caused it—Officer Rosmus—showed up at her house. She was sure the officer wanted to ensure that Mick hadn't seen her there, but it was all speculation, really. All she had was the video from Officer Rosmus's house with Brad's body in the freezer. She had no other evidence. She'd have to get the officer to confess, but that would be unlikely.

"Mick!" Sara yelled, which seemed to snap her friend out of his daze.

Mick blinked before focusing on Sara's face, but she didn't say anything. She just stood there, gazing at Sara as if she were seeing her for the first time.

"Mick, let's sit down," Sara suggested as she guided Mick to the sofa where she had just been seated moments earlier. She assisted Mick in sitting while keeping a hand on her arm. Sara smiled, and Mick returned the smile. "Should I call Mabel?"

"What? No, I'm fine, really. It's nice of you to come and see me, but I'm feeling tired now and should lie down," Mick said.

It confused Sara. *Lie down?* She had just arrived, and

now Mick wanted her to leave. Something wasn't right with Mick. Yes, she'd had a tragic experience, but she was home now and safe. Mick had nothing to worry about, yet deep inside, Sara struggled to believe that was true. She herself wasn't even safe. Maybe it was best that she left Mick's home and never returned. Would it protect her from something bad happening? This, Sara didn't know, but it was the only thing she felt she could do. But hadn't Officer Rosmus already been here? So, what difference did it make? If that witch could just show up whenever she wanted and continue to sink her claws into Mick, what good would it do to stay away?

Sara helped Mick to her bedroom and into bed. She pulled the blankets up just as Mick closed her eyes and felt Mick's breathing slow to a purr.

She stepped back and noticed several pill bottles on the nightstand. She picked one up; it read Zoloft. Was Mick taking an antidepressant? Though this shouldn't surprise her, it did. She unscrewed the lid and looked inside. There were a few pills left. How long had she been taking them? she seemed to ask herself. She picked up another bottle labeled Ritalin. Sara wasn't sure what those medications were for.

She put the pill bottles back on the nightstand and exited the room. She had to return to that cabin before daylight faded.

Chapter 53

She drove back toward the cabin and parked her car in the same spot as the night before. Once on the road, she turned right and headed toward the cabin. She knew it wasn't far from where she had parked, but she couldn't see the cabin from the road. With no other choice, she ventured into the woods until she found it.

Sara walked and walked, but still no cabin in sight. Had she taken the wrong road? No, she was certain she hadn't done that. And she was sure she hadn't imagined the whole thing, or at least hoped she hadn't. How did she end up turned around? She was positive it was the same road from last night.

She stopped and sat on an old, hollow stump. She could still see part of the road from where she sat, but there was no house. How could there not be a house? She had stood on the porch. She had looked inside the window. She hadn't made it all up. There was no freaking way!

She heard a vehicle approaching down the road. When the truck came into view, it moved slowly, as if searching for something. Then the truck stopped and turned left, bouncing as it drove through the woods on the opposite side from where she sat. It was the same truck she had seen many times before. It was Officer Rosmus, and the cabin was on the other side of the road.

Sara searched her mind, reflecting on last night. Had she parked in a different spot? Yes, that must be what she had done. It was dark last night, and this morning she had left going the other way. How could she have been so foolish? But now that she thought about it, if she'd been across the street, Rosmus would have found her.

From her vantage point, she could see when Officer Rosmus left the house, and then she could head to the cabin. Now, Sara was certain that something was over there. Maybe even someone.

She wasn't sure how long she had been sitting on the stump, watching and waiting for Officer Rosmus's truck to come out of the woods. She looked straight up through the tops of the trees and saw the light blue sky above. The sun was at high noon.

She heard an engine roar to life and then saw it emerge from behind the trees, turning right and barreling down the road away from the cabin. This was her chance to see what Rosmus was hiding.

Her legs felt stiff from sitting too long in the cold, but she stepped forward, placing one foot in front of the other. She couldn't afford to waste any more time than she already had.

Minutes later, she stood by the road, looked both ways, and then jogged across to the cabin. It was the same cabin she remembered from last night. However, somehow, it seemed different in the daylight. The wood that supported the cabin was a mossy, greenish-brown, giving it a weathered appearance. The windows were grimy, which was surprising considering how Rosmus's house looked. The woman was a clean freak, but just because the outside appeared dirty didn't mean the inside was.

She pulled her phone out and scrolled through the photos until she found the video she had taken at Rosmus's house. She fast-forwarded until she reached the image of the cabin. She studied the picture and looked up. Yep, it was the same house. She shoved the phone back into her coat pocket.

When she reached the steps, she looked down and noticed the dark green moss that she had seen and slipped on the previous night. This confirmed that she had been there. Feeling relieved, she walked up the steps and approached the door. She tried the handle, but just like the night before, it was locked.

She approached the window, shielding her eyes with a hand as she pressed her face against the glass. Everything appeared unchanged from the previous night, which further confirmed that she had not imagined any of it. She wasn't losing her mind.

Now that she could see everything, she scanned the moss-covered porch. There was no furniture or potted plants. Why would she think there would be? If someone like her had stumbled across this cabin, they would recognize that someone lived here if there was furniture and potted plants displayed.

She ran her hand along the door frame. No key. She then did the same above the window, coming up empty-handed. Turning, she jogged down the wooden stairs. This time, she went left instead of right. There had to be a way inside; she just didn't know where it was.

The branches crackled beneath her boots. She hadn't even attempted to be quiet. Why should she? There was no one out here who could hear her. Then it struck her. What if there was someone out here?

"Hello? Is anyone out here?" Sara called out. She stood still, listening intently.

Nothing.

There was no sound except for the wind rustling the skeletal branches around her. She called out again.

"Hello? If anyone is out here, please make some noise or holler."

It was faint, but she was sure she heard someone knocking on a wall inside the cabin.

"Keep knocking so I can find you," she said.

The knocking sound came again, and Sara moved toward it. It was coming from beneath the ground.

Chapter 54

Sara dropped to her knees and brushed away the leaves, but only found dirt. There was no trapdoor beneath the dirt, or at least not where she was standing.

"Keep making that sound," she shouted. She knew that if this person could hear her, then they had to be close.

She walked along the side of the house, listening for any noise, but she didn't hear anything. After walking around the entire perimeter, she ended up back where she had first heard the knocking sound. Imagining the layout of the house, she was certain there was a basement. This also meant that the only way to access it would be from inside the cabin. She had no choice but to break a window.

Her mind came up with various scenarios for getting inside the house. What if she parked her car behind the cabin and climbed through the window in the back? This way, no one would see it from the front. Especially if Rosmus showed up while she was inside. But wouldn't she leave tire tracks along the side? Unless the ground was frozen enough not to leave marks. She dug in the dirt. The ground wasn't frozen. She couldn't use her car.

"Screw it!" she muttered. "Who gives a shit about the damn window!" She had to get inside and save whoever was in there before Rosmus returned.

She rushed to the front of the house and up the steps. She used her elbow and slammed it into the glass, but it wouldn't break. She did it again until finally, the glass cracked.

She stepped back and used her boot to kick out the remaining pieces of the window. Glass shattered everywhere. She reached in and turned the lock, then pushed the window up and crawled through the opening. Glass crunched under her feet as she stood in the small, dainty kitchen.

"Hello," she hollered, the sound echoing through the house. "I'm here to help you. Can you hear me?" She heard the same knocking sound and followed it to a door near the back of the house that opened onto a steep flight of stairs. A flicker of a memory flooded her mind of when she was at Officer Rosmus's house and had fallen down the stairs in her basement. She couldn't think about that now. She had to find this person and get them out of here before Rosmus came back.

She felt along the wall for a switch but didn't find one. She would have to use her cell phone instead. Once she had light from her phone, she made her way down the cement steps, which felt more like entering an ancient tomb than a basement. When she reached the bottom, she moved the light around the small space, which was no bigger than an average-sized family room. Just like the officer's house, it was also pristine.

She noticed a door next to her and approached it. It was a large metal door, likely steel, featuring a latch across it. The latch had a lock—a lock that required a key.

"Shit!" she swore.

Officer Rosmus wasn't very trustworthy, but that shouldn't surprise her. She had been around Rosmus long enough to know that she kept things hidden. The necklace and the diary in Megan's room were also concealed. She didn't hide them very well, but they were still out of sight. The only reason Sara had found them was that she went snooping, which was exactly what she was doing at this very moment.

She raised a hand and banged on the door. She heard what sounded like a chair scraping across the floor. She searched her mind. Who could Rosmus have inside this room? Then it hit her. But she needed to be sure and not jump to conclusions.

She needed to find something to cut the lock off the door, but there was nothing down here.

"For crying out loud!" she shouted.

She ran back up the stairs to the first floor and into the kitchen. She opened drawer after drawer, searching for anything that could unlock the door or that she could use to cut the lock.

When she found nothing, she looked around the room and noticed a set of keys hanging near the front door, which she quickly grabbed. Why hadn't she checked there first? Well, she wasn't going to stand there and beat herself up over it. She needed to get back downstairs before Rosmus returned.

She dashed down the stairs, careful not to fall. If she got hurt, she would be of no use to the person locked behind the door. She set her cell phone on the floor with the light shining up so she could see. She tried each key, but so far, none of them worked. She was down to the last two keys when she heard the floorboards above her creak.

Chapter 55

She had nowhere to hide. Where was she going to go? They had made the stairs from cement instead of wood like most basement stairs. Her heart spasmed beneath her chest, and she was sure it was about to burst out and explode like fireworks on the Fourth of July.

She closed her eyes and took a breath. She slipped one of the two remaining keys into the lock and turned it. The lock came apart, and she quickly removed it from the latch and pulled the door open, but not before grabbing her cell phone from the floor.

She slipped inside, closing the door behind her. The room was dark. Keeping one hand on the door, she turned around. Shining the light from her phone in front of her, she saw not one but two people. One was Megan, who looked exactly like Robyn, the girl she had found dead in the woods.

She shined the light on the second person and saw an older woman. There was no doubt in her mind that this had to be Delaney, Officer Rosmus's sister. Questions formed in her mind about why they were down here, being held captive. None of this made sense to her. Why would Rosmus keep her niece and sister hostage in this room? And not just any room, but in a cabin in the woods that no one seemed to know about.

Sara snapped out of her thoughts, walked over to Megan, and removed the gag from around her head and mouth, then untied her arms from behind the chair. Then I moved to Delaney, who was tied to the bed with her arms above her head. She also had a gag in her mouth.

"How long have you both been down here?" Sara asked.

"I'm not sure, maybe a couple of weeks," Megan replied.

Sara nodded. She knew who they were, but still didn't understand why they were down here. What did they know about Officer Rosmus that made her feel the need to tie them up and lock them in this room?

Sara helped Delaney sit up as the door opened behind her, and she sensed a presence in the doorway. Dread and fear coursed through her body. She didn't want to turn around and see Officer Rosmus there, but she felt compelled to look. Although she felt nauseous, she also experienced relief when she saw Reece standing in the open doorway instead of Officer Rosmus.

"Oh, my God," Sara mumbled as she stood beside Delaney. "I'm so glad that it's you and not her."

She could have sworn he muttered the words, *"What the hell!"*, but she couldn't be sure.

"Megan," Reece said, glancing at Delaney. "What the? Did Crystal do this to you?"

"Yes," Delaney replied in a raspy voice. "After you left that night, when we found out about her kidnapping Megan from the hospital when she was a baby, she knocked me over the head, and the next thing I knew, I was here in this room."

"Yeah, and then she came after me. That's how I broke my leg," Megan said.

Sara looked around the room and saw the pink coat she had noticed on that rainy night. She then glanced at Megan and down at her right leg, which wore a black boot. How had she not noticed that when she entered the room? Well, it was dark, and all she had was the light from her cell phone.

"You," Sara whispered. "It was you that I saw on the road that night."

Megan looked at Sara, her eyes wide with recognition.

"I was trying to help you, but when I turned back around, you had disappeared."

Megan nodded.

"Why? Was she chasing you, Officer Rosmus?" Sara asked.

"Yes."

"Let's ask questions later. We need to get them out of here before Crystal comes back," Reece said.

Reece gathered Megan into his arms while Sara wrapped an arm around Delaney and helped her up the stairs to the first floor. Both Megan and Delaney were safely in Reece's pickup truck when Officer Rosmus arrived.

Rosmus's truck came to an abrupt stop several feet from where they stood. Rosmus jumped out of her vehicle. "What the hell do you think you're doing?" she shouted as she stormed over to where Reece stood.

"Crystal, why? Is it all because of what you did? Because you kidnapped Megan, and we found out?" Reece asked.

"They would turn me in. I couldn't let them. I'm a respected officer in this town. They would have taken my badge!" Officer Rosmus shouted. "I would go to jail. Worse prison!"

Reece shook his head. "Delaney's your sister, and Megan, she's just a kid. How long did you think you could keep them locked up down there?"

"As long as I had to. I had to keep them from telling

anyone what I had done all those years ago," Rosmus stammered.

"Did you kill Robyn too? And go after Abby?" Reece asked.

"No, I had nothing to do with Robyn's death. She wasn't even at the house after you left. She said she had to attend to something and left. I honestly thought she had left town again. She was nothing but a nobody, a runaway," Rosmus replied, her nostrils flaring. "As for Abby, she said that she was hit over the head and was going to be buried." Rosmus nodded in Sara's direction. "She's the one who found her in that house. The Tanner house. Why don't you ask her those questions? Maybe she's the one who tried to kill her."

The accusation shocked Sara. Officer Rosmus was trying to pin everything on Sara, who hadn't arrived until after it had all happened. Abby had said that Robyn tried to kill her, but Sara was still a bit confused about Megan and Delaney's situation. However, now wasn't the time to sort it all out. They needed to get both Megan and Delaney to the hospital.

"Take my truck and get them out of here. Take them to the hospital," Reece demanded.

"What about you?" Sara asked.

Reece replied, "I'm taking Crystal to the police station and turning her in."

"Oh no, you're not," Rosmus shouted as she drew the gun from her holster and aimed it at them.

Reece stepped in front of Sara. "Crystal, you don't want to do this," Reece said.

"Yes, I do. I will not let you take me in."

Sara saw Delaney climb out of the truck, holding a crowbar in her hand. Delaney raised the crowbar into the air just as Rosmus turned around and the gun went off.

Chapter 56

Sara saw everything in slow motion as the scene replayed repeatedly in her mind. Delaney raised the crowbar, and then the gun fired. Delaney collapsed onto the thick carpet of pine needles and branches covering the ground, a bullet hole in her chest. Blood seeped through her blouse as she lay on the ground, with Megan by her side.

"Oh, my God!" Rosmus shouted. "Look what you made me do!"

Reece grabbed Officer Rosmus's arm and twisted it back, causing the gun to fall from her hand to the ground. Sara ran over and snatched the gun out of the officer's reach.

Rosmus howled as tears streamed down her face. "Oh, Delaney," she cried, struggling to break free from Reece's grasp. Reece released her, and Rosmus collapsed to the ground beside her sister.

"I'm so sorry, Delaney. I'm so terribly sorry," she wept. "I never meant for it to go this far. Please don't you die on me." Officer Rosmus bowed her head and rested it on Delaney's chest.

Sara saw Rosmus's body shaking as she cried. She handed the gun to Reece and stood next to him while he called the local police.

By the time the ambulance arrived, Delaney had died.

Minutes later, Sheriff White arrived with two other police officers and arrested Officer Rosmus for the death of her sister, Delaney, as well as for kidnapping Megan when she was a baby and again two weeks ago.

Sheriff White questioned Sara, who informed him about her boyfriend Brad's body being in a freezer located in Officer Rosmus's garage. She also showed Sheriff White and the others the video she had recorded.

"I think she may have also killed Edith and Steve, the man you found upstairs," Sara stated.

Sheriff White nodded, writing down everything that Sara said. "We got the results back in Edith's death, and it showed that she died of asphyxiation. Someone had killed her; we just don't have all the evidence yet. Something we will have to investigate. As for Steve, I'll have to check into that. Rosmus was handling most of the cases, so now I must have the files rechecked," Sheriff White said. "I have no doubt she has tampered with the evidence to cover her tracks. We'll need to check everything she oversaw."

Sara nodded in agreement, her heart feeling lighter than it had in the past few days since Edith's death. Once she finished being questioned, she walked away. It took her a few minutes to reach her car, which she had parked down the road. She wasn't in any hurry; after all, the one person she had feared was dead and had been for… well, she wasn't sure how long Brad had been gone. As for Officer Rosmus, she wouldn't pose a problem anymore either.

She climbed into her car and started the engine, but she didn't leave. Not because the engine needed to warm up first, but because something caught her eye. The necklace that she had hung around the rearview mirror was missing. She hadn't realized when it had gone. Had Rosmus taken the necklace from her car and placed it back in Megan's jewelry box? This was possible, and she would have to ask, but did it matter anymore? Megan was now free. What would happen to her now, Sara didn't know.

Her thoughts turned to Mick and how she had acted when Sara visited her before coming here. It was something Mick had said to her, but it hadn't registered until now. Sara shifted into drive and stepped on the gas. She raced out of the woods and headed toward Mick's apartment, praying that she would get there in time.

A few minutes later, Sara parked the car and dashed to the door of the apartment building. She pressed every button until someone buzzed her in. When the door clicked, she pulled it open and raced up the stairs. She turned the knob on the door, relieved that it wasn't locked. She hurried to Mick's bedroom and found her in the bed where she had left her.

The pill bottles were still sitting beside the bed. Earlier, when Sara was here, the date on the bottle read four days ago. If that was the case, why were there only a few pills left inside the bottle?

Sara shook Mick, but she lay unresponsive. She placed two fingers on Mick's neck. His pulse was faint. She pulled out her cell phone and dialed for help, but she wasn't sure if they would make it to her in time. She couldn't let Mick die like Delaney had at the hands of Officer Rosmus.

Sara pulled Mick into the bathroom and forced her fingers down his throat until she threw up into the toilet.

✣ ✣ ✣

Two days later, Sara sat beside Mick's hospital bed. She hadn't left Mick's side since she had found her at home, nearly dead. Sara didn't want to leave until Mick woke up, confident that her friend would be okay.

Sara turned to look at Mabel, who was sleeping in the chair against the wall. It was late, close to midnight, when Mick opened her eyes. Her throat sounded hoarse as she spoke.

"Sara?" Mick questioned, looking so small and fragile, lying in the hospital bed.

Sara told Mick everything that had happened over the past couple of days, and she was also right about Officer Rosmus trying to kill Mick.

"Was it him in that house the night I ran outside?"

"No, it had been Officer Rosmus, according to Sheriff White. Brad's body had been dead for at least ten days, maybe more. Evidence on the pillow in Edith's bedroom came back with Officer Rosmus's DNA all over it, which was probably why she had gone back into Edith's room later that day. I'm surprised she hadn't thought about the pillow and disposed of it. They also found the hammer used on Steve at the bottom of the freezer, where she kept Brad's body. Rosmus was eliminating people she thought were suspicious of her. Possibly, they had known about what she had done to Megan and Delaney, people who had arrived in town. She would have gotten you, too, if you hadn't run out of the house that night," Sara said. "I'm just surprised she hadn't killed me. I'm not sure what she was waiting for?"

"Oh, my God," Mick replied as a tear escaped and slid down her face, landing on the soft white pillow beneath her head. "I've known Rosmus for years. I… I can't believe she's a monster. She was at my house right before you that day. She made me swallow a bunch of pills. I…" Mick cried harder. "I don't know what I was thinking. I'm so sorry."

"No, I'm sorry, Mick." Sara reached out and squeezed

Mick's arm. "She'll never hurt you again. I promise."

Sara was leaving town tonight and returning home, where she belonged. Craven Falls was not a place she wanted to live, even though she was confident that there would be no more deaths or killings now that Officer Rosmus was behind bars.

Chapter 57

Sara exited the hospital and got into her car. She drove to the police station in town and parked. There was one more thing she needed to find out before she left town for good.

She sat in the small, confined room where she was sure they interrogated criminals—just like the one she was about to talk to. The door opened, and Officer Rosmus shuffled inside. They handcuffed both her ankles and wrists. The male officer placed Rosmus in a chair at the table, turned, closed the door, and waited outside in the hallway.

"What the hell do you want?" Rosmus finally asked.

"I just have a couple of questions that I need answered before I leave town."

"Like what? What do you need to know? Brad? He was a son of a bitch to kill, I'll give you that much. Put up a hell of a fight. Initially, I wasn't sure why he was here, but after observing him for a day, it became clear that he was searching for you. Shit, I should've had him just kill you. Then I would've gotten away with everything. I was such a stupid fool. But he got what he deserved in the end. Did you do a favor if you ask me?" Rosmus said.

"Yes, you did, but why did you kill him?"

"He was obstructing the way. He wasn't going to leave town quietly. I saw an opportunity, and I took it. Again, I did you a favor by killing him."

"And Steve? Who was he? Why was he here in Craven

Falls?" Sara asked.

Rosmus shook her head before bursting into a deep belly laugh. "Why do you want to know about that guy? God, he was just as much trouble as Brad."

Sara shrugged her shoulders. "Just need to know what he was in town for."

"Well, it wasn't you he was here for, if that's what you're worried about."

"So, then tell me why," Sara pressed.

"That guy used to work for Mr. Fitzgerald. He did some work for him on the side."

"And?"

"And what?"

"God, why do you have to make this so hard?" Sara asked.

Rosmus growled before speaking. "Fine. He was sent to kill Ken Tanner, which he did. I found him and his wife's bodies in the shed behind their house two weeks ago. They were shot in the head and left bound and gagged in the shed behind their house."

Sara searched her mind for the day she had first gone to the Tanner house when she found Robyn's body in the woods. She had seen the shed sitting to the right in the backyard. She shivered at the thought of them being dead inside for how long she didn't know. "Why did he kill them? I mean, you said he worked for Mr. Fitzgerald, so why did he want them dead?" Sara asked.

"Ken knew about the mayor."

"Mayor?"

"Yes, Mr. Fitzgerald was the mayor of Craven Falls. Ken found evidence that the mayor doctored the files when his wife killed two locals here in Craven Falls. He covered up the accident with false information. Ken Tanner planned to go to Sheriff White and turn him in. According to Steve, Fitzgerald wanted Ken dead. Coincidentally, Cheryl was there too. So, as the saying goes, he killed two birds with one stone. I guess he figured, why not kill them both and be done with it."

"I don't know. It seems like there should be more of a reason than the fact that Mr. Fitzgerald doctored some files," Sara stated.

"Well, you're a nosy bitch, aren't you? Fine! Before I killed Steve, he said that Ken Tanner and Martha Fitzgerald were having an affair. That Mr. Fitzgerald wanted him dead. She was coming home from Ken's house when she got into the accident that killed the other two people. She was high on cocaine. Said that it would've ruined the mayor's chances of reelection, so he had the statement changed on the cause of the accident," Rosmus said. "So, to shut Ken's mouth before word got out, he had him killed, and you know the rest."

Sara leaned back in the chair, absorbing the words she had just heard. This town was heading for disaster even before she had arrived. But there was a reason she had taken that road, leading her to this town two weeks ago. That reason was to save Megan and Delaney from Rosmus, although Delaney had ultimately died, with no help from her sister.

There was nothing left to do now. Everything she wanted to know had been answered, and she could return home to the life she once had before Brad destroyed everything.

About the Author

Donna M. Zadunajsky is an award-winning author who began her writing career with children's books before publishing her first novel, *Broken Promises*, in June 2012. She has since written several more novels and her first novella, *HELP ME!*, which addresses the topics of teen suicide and bullying.

To find out more about the author, go to: http://www.donnazadunajsky.com.

More books by Donna M. Zadunajsky

Novels

Broken Promises

Not Forgotten

The Accident

Secrets and Second Chances Series

Family Secrets- Book 1

Hidden Secrets- Book 2

Twisted Secrets- Book 3

Young Adult

Craven Falls Series

The Dead Girl Under the Bleachers- Book 1

Buried Secrets- Book 2

The Body in the Road- Book 3

Novellas

HELP ME Series

HELP ME! -Book 1

TALK TO ME -Book 2

www.ingramcontent.com/pod-product-compliance
Lightning Source LLC
Chambersburg PA
CBHW010142030826
48979CB00028B/2149/J

* 9 7 8 1 9 3 8 0 3 7 8 1 8 *